Puffin Books
Editor: Kaye Webb
The Horsemasters

Twenty past six in the morning, and the alarm clock
ringing! It was almost enough to make Dinah give up
horses for good, especially as that bell was the signal for
mucking out Cornish Pasty, the messiest horse in the
stables, and all before she had had a bite to eat herself.
Looking back on it, though, Dinah could see how that
early-morning drill had helped to turn a disorganized band
of riding school recruits into an experienced, disciplined
team who would keep up the pace and high standards all
day, however much they disliked Mercy, the tough
unfriendly head girl who kept them so hard at work.
Since Dinah had come to join the Horsemasters to learn
to ride, she'd learned that there was much more to horses
than jumping and galloping about.

But, work over, how great were the joys of learning a new
technique in dressage, controlling a horse with aids so
slight that they were almost invisible, of understanding
a horse better than ever before! Dinah had never found
riding so satisfying and thrilling, or enjoyed herself so
much in a group of friendly, like-minded people.
    No one could read this book without responding to the
devotion and enthusiasm of the characters and learning a
lot about horses.

Don Stanford

The Horsemasters

Puffin Books

Puffin Books,
Penguin Books Ltd,
Harmondsworth, Middlesex, England
Penguin Books,
625 Madison Avenue, New York, New York 10022
Penguin Books Australia Ltd,
Ringwood, Victoria, Australia
Penguin Books Canada Ltd,
41 Steelcase Road West, Markham, Ontario, Canada
Penguin Books (N.Z.) Ltd,
182–190 Wairau Road, Auckland 10, New Zealand

First published by Brockhampton Press 1956
Published in Puffin Books 1976
Copyright © Don Stanford, 1956

Made and printed in Great Britain by
Hazell Watson & Viney Ltd,
Aylesbury, Bucks
Set in Linotype Baskerville

Contents

For George Cole Toomey, *Horseman*

Chapter 1

Early Stables

In the warm, dark, quiet depths of sleep, the shrill, persistent ringing was a rude intruder. It was a distant telephone, and someone else would answer it ... or it was a school bell, signifying the end of a class period – for someone else. No, it was a telephone, and *why* didn't somebody answer the thing and stop that horrible noise so a person could go on sleeping, peaceful and snug and warm ... ?

The ringing continued, rudely and unpleasantly and seeming to grow nearer and louder, and at last Dinah Wilcox could no longer pretend it was anything but an alarm clock. *Her* alarm clock. Groaning, she burrowed her face deeper into the pillows and stretched out one arm to feel around on the bedside table until she found the clock and stilled its clamour with a vindictive bang. But the clock continued to tick loudly and imperturbably until Dinah opened one sleepy brown eye and glowered balefully at its round bland face, which informed her smugly that it was twenty minutes past six o'clock in the morning.

'Oh, shut *up!*' Dinah muttered at the clock. The world outside the open window was still light grey in colour, moist and gloomy and a little chilly from the night. Dinah shuddered and wriggled down into the warmth of the bed resolutely shutting her eyes tight and clinging to a few more seconds of sleep. But she could not shut out the loud ticking of the clock, and now she began to hear sounds of life along the hall. Some of the others were already up; *somebody* must be dressed already, and clumping around with boots on ...

With a sudden convulsive effort of will, Dinah erupted out of bed in a leap to stand shivering on the bare floor. She glared at the tangled mass of black hair barely visible between the drawn-up quilt and the pillow of the next bed and commanded sternly.

'Beatrice Byington Simms, *get up*!'

There was no response at all from the motionless bulge beneath the covers, and Dinah urged a little more loudly:

'Bee Bye! Come on, Bee Bye; get up, Bee Bye! It's six-twenty, Bee Bye; get *up*, girl!'

Bee Bye groaned and shook her head, burying her face more deeply in the pillow and dragging the quilt up until she disappeared entirely. Dinah said, loudly and clearly:

'Okay, sleep. *Get* left with a mucksack with a hole in the middle and a busted pitchfork and a shovel that won't shove and a broom with no bristles. *I* should worry. I'm leaving. G'bye.'

She gathered up soap, towel, and toothbrush and made for the hall and the bathroom beyond; as she passed Bee Bye's bed she casually grabbed a corner of the sheet and with one deft yank stripped all the bed-clothes to the floor. Then she fled, giggling, with Bee Bye's shriek of anguished fury ringing in her ears.

Eight minutes later Dinah clattered downstairs in faded jeans and a boy's shirt, with her cropped mouse-blonde hair still tousled, and headed at a brisk trot for the stables. She hardly noticed the fresh early-morning smell of grass still wet with dew, or the beauty of the green paddocks stretching down to the grey sea, or the neat peaceful hedgerows of the English countryside; her awakening mind was now on the business at hand. *Horses*.

Racing into the brick-paved stable yard, still glistening wet from the dew, she could hear them stamping and pawing restlessly as they awakened; she could smell them, too, and she drew in the deepest breath she could hold, filling her nostrils with the wonderful exhilarating stable smell of sweet hay and ammonia and warm, strong life ... *horses*! She caught a fleeting glimpse of a grey rump and a bay one, both black tails swishing, as she raced past the open door behind which were the five standing stalls of Stable One. Nightingale and Pennant, and nobody down to take care of *them* yet ... These standing stalls, in which the horses were tied, were much smaller than the loose boxes in which they were untied and could walk around. In one of the loose boxes in Stable Two a horse kicked shatteringly as she passed, and Dinah shouted at him:

'Cotton Socks! You stop that! Your Mama's on her way!'

She skidded into Stable Three, past the loose box just inside the door, ducking as the tall chestnut horse in the loose box stretched his neck over the bar and reached for a mouthful of her hair. The black horse in the end standing stall was standing squarely in the middle of his stall with one white hind foot cocked negligently up on its toe and his weight resting on the other; Dinah gave his muscular rump a solid slap as she squeezed between the horse and the wall of the stall to find the water bucket lying on its side in a welter of wet mussed straw beneath his manger. The black horse was a tough old cob named Cornish Pasty; he was ugly and clumsy and ungainly, and in the course of the night he had as usual managed not only to upset his water bucket but to muss and soil almost all the straw in his stall into a wild, smelly disarray. Dinah gave the filthy stall a rueful glance as she stooped to pick up the water bucket; Cornish Pasty craned his neck and nuzzled her with an inquiring black nose, and she patted his neck absently and murmured mournfully:

'Oh, Corny P., you *are* the untidiest horse!'

She hurried out to set the water bucket on the upside-down zinc trough in the stable yard and let cold fresh water splash into it from the gleaming brass tap above. As she waited for the bucket to fill, Sally Burnham sauntered out of Stable One negligently swinging Nightingale's bucket, and for the thousandth time Dinah thought wistfully how wonderful it would be to have Nightingale to take care of, instead of old Corny P. The beautiful little grey Arab was dainty and neat and no trouble at all; Sally could muck out his stall in the mornings in half the time it took Dinah to clean up after Corny. She dragged the heavy bucket off the trough as Sally slid hers into its place, murmuring to the big girl:

'Morning, Sally. Want to trade Nitty for Corny, just for today?'

'What a hope!' Sally snorted, and brayed with laughter.

Morosely, Dinah lugged the water bucket off; Roger Nicholson was just coming through the yard door into the stable yard, lugging an armload of mucksacks, pitchforks, shovels, and brooms. He gave her his wonderful warm grin and managed somehow to free two fingers and hold them up, indicating that he had two of everything.

'I've got Adrienne's!' Roger stage-whispered and winked, 'Morning, Dinah!'

'Morning, Rog,' Dinah answered, wishing she could feel as wonderful as Roger evidently did in the mornings. But then Roger was a farm boy from the Isle of Wight; he was used to getting up at crack of dawn and taking care of animals ... She squeezed past Corny P. and plunked his bucket down in the straw beneath the manger; as he lowered his old black head and plunged his nose eagerly into it to drink, she slipped out again and ran through the yard door. From the clothes-line by the muck heap she picked a mucksack, a simple four-foot square of burlap made by cutting open an old feed sack; from the shed she got a pitchfork, shovel, and broom. It was the last shovel there was, and the edge was worn and crumpled; there were more brooms, but all the good ones had been taken. As she raced back to Corny's stall she saw Bee Bye Simms skidding into the stable yard and derisively brandished her armload of tools. Poor Bee Bye would have heavy going this morning . . .

Spreading the mucksack carefully on the concrete floor behind Corny's stall, Dinah took up her pitchfork and began clearing the straw away from the front corner opposite the manger. When she had a clear square yard of floor, she swept it thoroughly and then began to fork what dry clean straw she could find into a heap there, tossing wet and soiled straw to the back of the stall. She worked feverishly, trying to have a clean place for Corny to stand while he ate his breakfast; she would finish the mucking out while he ate, but it would be time to feed him in just a couple of minutes now.

The others were all down now; without looking up from her work Dinah could sense them coming and going busily. For every one of the fourteen horses in these three stables there was one girl or boy working as hard and as fast as he could to care for that horse in accordance with the School's strict, high standards. Except, of course, for the calf-kneed little chestnut in the end stall, the gelding called Nutmeg.

Dinah straightened and craned for a hasty glance at the back of Nutmeg's stall and saw the mucksack neatly spread out there with a half-load of soiled straw and droppings piled neatly in its middle and the pitchfork leaning alongside as though Adrienne had just set it down for a minute to do something else. *Good old Roger!* Dinah thought, and giggled; sooner or later poor Adrienne would get caught oversleeping as she did every single morning, but up to now they were getting away with protecting the little Swiss girl from the wrath of Mercy

Hale. And it was fun, putting something over on the Head Girl.

'*Fee-eed!*' Mercy was shrilling now, banging on the feed bin and making a horrible din. Corny P. threw his head up, snorting, and rolled his eyes wildly; he stamped and danced clumsily round to crowd against the front of his stall, sideways, where he could watch the stable entrance.

Dinah ducked under his belly and dashed out to the feed bin where the others were already forming a ragged queue, a forlorn lot of drowsy kids in frayed and sloppy dungarees, their faces still numb with sleep. Jill Taylor was at the end of the line, and the plump Scots girl was carrying two feed buckets; Dinah picked up the best one of those that were left and fell in behind Jill. Bee Bye Simms sprinted out of Stable Two, grabbed a bucket, and stood close behind Dinah, grumbling:

'The most famous riding school in England, and supposed to be the best, and they can't provide enough tools to go round ... *huh*! I swear, I'm going to *buy* a shiny new shovel and a broom, all for myself, and keep 'em locked up where nobody else can get at 'em.'

'Not in *our* closet, you're not!' Dinah told her firmly and added heartlessly, 'If you'd try getting up just above five minutes earlier in the morning, you might not get left with the last-choice tools every day ... You can have my shovel when I've finished mucking out, Bee Bye.'

'Thanks!' Bee Bye muttered sarcastically. 'You've only got the filthiest horse in the place. It shouldn't take you much past breakfast time. I'll borrow –'

'Adrienne!' Mercy Hale called sharply and raised her thin voice and repeated, '*Adrienne!* Has anyone seen Adrienne? Has Nutmeg been watered?'

'Oh, yes, Mercy!' Dinah called sweetly. 'Nutmeg's been watered and partly mucked out; I just saw –'

'She's filling our hay nets,' Jill Taylor lied blandly, looking Mercy straight in the eye and rattling her two buckets together. 'I'll feed for both of us. This bucket for Nutmeg, and this one for Shadow, please.'

Without a word and with only a second's hesitation, Mercy dished up oats into the two buckets, but the tight-closed suspicious expression was still on her face as plump Jill swaggered away. Mercy Hale was tiny. She had beautiful, almost-white blonde hair and a small, delicate blue-eyed face, and it was the unanimous opinion of the students taking the Owen-Allerford Riding School's Horsemastership Course that Mercy Hale was tough as a turtle and mean as a snake.

'Cornish Pasty,' Dinah said crisply, and Mercy dumped in a measure of oats. Dinah stepped round Mercy's small square-shouldered form and leaned over the chaff bin to scoop a double handful into the bucket on top of Corny P.'s oats; as she carried the bucket back to the stall, she stirred the oats and chaff together with her hand.

Corny P. came charging round against the side of his stall the way he did every morning, frantic with hunger; Dinah was no longer afraid that he would squash her flat against the boards in the process. She dumped his feed into the manger, and as he began to eat greedily, she caught up her pitchfork and feverishly began to throw soiled straw and manure on to the mucksack spread out behind his stall. When the heap was high enough, she gathered up the four corners of the burlap square and with an effort heaved the heavy, smelly load on to her back; bent double beneath her burden, she plodded out of the stable yard and down the path towards the muck heap, mentally ticking off the things she would have to do, on the double, in the hour and three-quarters between now and breakfast. Three more loads like this, and Corny's stall would be clean; then lug a bale of straw down from the barn and spread it evenly over the stall floor, piling it up in the corners and along the sides ...

'Hi, Dynamite!' David Perrin greeted her as he passed, and Dinah smiled up at the slender, red-headed young man from beneath her burden. David was a little older than the rest of the Horsemasters; he was twenty-three, and he was a magnificent horseman, nearly as good as the instructors; probably he had a perfect right to be a little condescending to the others. It certainly infuriated Bee Bye, though, and Bee Bye was the only one David *didn't* condescend to; Bee Bye had been riding all her life and was practically in his class, and David always tried to be friendly with her, but he got only cold hostility for his pains.

... And then, Dinah thought, picking up where she had left off at David's passing, Corny would have finished his breakfast and she could start grooming him. Half an hour for that, to do a job Mercy wouldn't find fault with. Then twenty minutes of strapping, banging him all over with a block of plaited hay until her arms ached, to harden his muscles and stimulate his circulation. Then hop to and wash down the stable yard ...

Mercy Hale was waiting at the muck heap; the girl seemed to be everywhere. She said curtly:

'Dinah, you've got a hole in your mucksack; you've dribbled straw all along the path. Make sure it's all swept up before you go up to breakfast.'

Muttering resentfully under her breath, Dinah dumped her load and hurried back for more. Adrienne was at work now, drowsily throwing straw out of Nutmeg's stall and looking helpless and pathetic huddled in an old ski jacket far too large for her. The little Swiss girl had been sent to Owen-Allerford School primarily to improve her English, she explained, although her father wanted her to be able to take care of her own horse when she got home to

Lausanne. And although she was placid and sweet and very pretty with her black hair and dark-blue eyes, Adrienne was having a hard time. She obviously hadn't ever done anything remotely resembling work in her life before, and this was hard work; also, she frequently misunderstood commands and brought down the screaming wrath of the instructors upon her uncomprehending head, and she could *not* get up on time in the mornings. But the others all liked Adrienne and conspired to help and protect her.

Corny P.'s stall was immaculate at last, and he had finished his feed. Dinah got the coarse dandy brush out of her grooming kit, and he turned his head to look at her, his eyes half-closed with drowsy, pleasurable anticipation. Corny loved being groomed. Dinah put her arms round his neck and leaned against him for a moment, laying her face against his warm, sleek neck and breathing in his nice horsy smell; then she began to brush him vigorously all over with the dandy brush, excepting only his tail. The dandy brush could split the hairs of a horse's mane or tail and was never used there. But Corny didn't have a mane; his was clipped close to his neck ... She threw the dandy brush back into her kit and got out the fine, flat body brush and curry-comb and began to go over him again thoroughly, drawing the brush through the teeth of the curry-comb at the end of each firm stroke to clean it, and never touching his body with the comb at all. His glossy black body was shining when she had finished; she went over him once more with a stable rubbing cloth like a dish towel to put a finishing high sheen on his coat.

She stood back a moment to admire her work, and as the horse turned his head to look at her again, she murmured:

'You're *beautiful*, Corny P., just simply beautiful!'

Corny looked away, pleased and embarrassed; he

shuffled his feet, being unable to blush. Dinah giggled and briskly got back to business. She moistened her sponge and carefully cleaned out his eyes and nostrils; Corny squeezed his eyes tight shut like a baby to have his face washed, but he ducked his head down so she could reach it easily, and he wore a ludicrous expression of pleasure on his ugly, enormous, Roman-nosed old black face. She patted his nose and skipped back to sponge his dock; then she tossed the sponge back into her grooming kit and stood close behind him with the rolled tail bandage in her hand. She draped his tail over her shoulder and very carefully wound the bandage round it in a neat tight spiral, and gave the tail a quick crimp when she had finished.

'All right, Bub!' she murmured, stooping, and as she lightly tapped his fetlock, Cornish Pasty obediently lifted his hoof to be picked out. But as soon as she took hold of it, he put his weight against her hand; muttering imprecations under her breath, Dinah strained with all her strength to hold the hoof off the ground long enough to scrape it clean with the steel hook of her hoof pick.

'Just sit down and take him on your lap, why not?' a voice bubbling with laughter advised, and Dinah raised a flushed face to the sparkling impish one of Peanuts Pride, leaning like a jaunty elf on the handle of her pitchfork. 'That's all he wants, y'know, a little maternal tenderness!'

'This – this old black hippopotamus!' Dinah said with bitterness. 'Just look at that hoof – the size of a soup plate! And if there's any dirt around, he'll step in it and then knock me flat on my back while I'm trying to clean it out for him ... I *do* wish I could swap for some nice clean normal horse for a while. Like Nightingale, or –'

'Trade you Pipe Clay!' Peanuts offered promptly, and Dinah shuddered.

'No, *thanks!*' she said hastily, 'not *that* old cannibal! Horrible as he is, at least old Corny P. doesn't *bite* everybody within reach ... do you, Baby?' she crooned, patting Corny's flank as she moved round to pick up the other hind foot.

'Well ...' Peanuts said, lingering. 'I only wanted to be helpful, y'know!'

'Y'didn't, y'know!' Dinah responded promptly, and Peanuts instantly repeated, giggling:

'I *did*, y'know!'

'Y'*didn't*, y'know!' Dinah said again, mimicking Mr Ffolliott, the old horse trainer from whom all the Horse-masters had picked up the expression. They laughed together, and Dinah added ruefully, 'Y'know, there *is* a certain amount of work involved in taking care of a horse, isn't there?'

'There *is*, y'know!' Peanuts agreed with feeling and ran a hand through her mop of auburn curls. 'If I'd had any *idea* how much personal service the tyrannical things demand every single day, I'd 've pestered Father for a car instead of a show-jumper. A nice, quiet, uncomplaining little car that would just sit quietly in the garage until you wanted to use it, never mussing up its stall or dirtying its tack or having to be fed and watered three times a day, not to mention having its bedpan emptied ... But I loved riding at school, and it was the only sport I was ever any good at, so when Father asked what I'd like for a graduation present, of course I promptly said a good show-jumper. And how was I to know, when he coughed and said all right, if I took the Horsemastership Course and passed, and still wanted to own a horse and take care of it myself.... ?'

Dinah lowered Corny P.'s last clean foot to the floor and slipped past him to toss her hoof pick back into the grooming kit and pick up her hay wisp. Laughing at Peanuts's mournful expression, she agreed, 'Bee Bye was counting it up last night in the Blue Room; I don't know where you were. It adds up to over three hours a day we spend on stable work and grooming, not counting cleaning tack or yards and brasses or anything like that. And it has to be spread over thirteen hours between morning feed and night watering, which makes it kind of confining, to say the least. And we only ride two hours a day ... Jiggers, *Mercy*!'

Peanuts fled, nearly colliding with Mercy Hale as she shot through the door and out of Stable Three. Dinah turned quickly to stand square to Cornish Pasty's shoulder; he flinched and braced himself as she drew back the block of plaited hay and blinked as she hit him with all her strength, drew back and hit him again, rhythmically. Mercy Hale came and stood silently at the back of the stall, and without looking at Mercy, Dinah continued to strap Corny P., putting all her weight behind each solid blow on his neck, his shoulders, his legs and quarters and back. Corny's ugly old black face wore an expression of sheer bliss; this, to him, was a luxurious massage, it toned up his circulation and turned all his fat to hard muscle, and it felt *good*.

Mercy turned away and left without saying a word, and Dinah eased up a little in the force of her blows; her arm was beginning to ache, and before she had finished, it would feel as though it were dropping off ... and then, before she had quite finished, Mercy was banging on the feed box again, calling in her high, piping voice:

'Yards, please; yards, everybody!'

Dinah gave Corny P. three final solid bangs on his rump and tossed the hay wisp into her grooming kit; quickly she threw a light rug over him, fastened it over his chest and buckled the stable roller round him. She gave his stall one swift, checking glance, and her eyes widened in horror; she caught up her empty hay net and ran like a rabbit. Fill that net before the stable yard was swept was the rule, or sweep the yard again yourself ... and already there were ragged, shabby figures emerging from all the stables, trailing brooms in response to Mercy's clarion call.

She dived into the hay barn, thankful that someone had left most of an open bale; throwing herself to her knees in the fragrant hay, she began to scrabble and stuff it into the netting sack with both hands. She ran again, with the bulging sack over her shoulder; just in time.

David and Roger and Adrienne and Jill were sweeping, advancing over the brick expanse of the stable yard in a military line with their brooms swinging in unison; Bee Bye and Peanuts had righted the zinc trough and were standing by it with buckets while it filled. Dinah could hear the others, the Horsemasters of Red Ride, busily sweeping the paths and drives beyond the stable yard as she hung up Corny's hay net and grabbed a bucket to join Bee Bye at the trough.

And then, as the sweepers reached the end of the yard and turned back, Bee Bye and Peanuts and Dinah spilled bucketful after bucketful of cold, clear water in great, spreading, splashing lakes on to the bricks just ahead of the swinging brooms, and the brooms caught greedily at the spreading water and chased it ahead of them, with the last tiny bits of straw and dirt bobbing helplessly on its surface ... And at last the whole expanse of brick glistened wet and immaculate and somehow the work was all done, and there wasn't anything more to do but put the tools away ... and a great booming gong was sounding from Allerford House, and Mercy Hale was shrilling:

'All right, breakfast; breakfast, everybody!'

And Dinah Wilcox, straightening her aching back and curling her toes inside chilly wet socks, decided that she had never in her entire life been as hungry as she was right now. There was a clatter of tools and a torrent of babbling voices as the kids from Red Ride came racing into the stable yard, and Dinah took one last, tingling, proud look at the gleaming perfection of the job in which she had done her part and turned and raced with the others to clean up and change clothes in the fifteen minutes before breakfast would be served.

Chapter 2

'Dumb But Determined'

The Horsemasters' dining-room looked out, through french windows open to the morning sunlight, over a stone terrace and a screen of rose-bushes to the terraced grassy paddocks rolling down to the sea. The dark-panelled room was a babble of eager voices and scraping chairs and clattering crockery, redolent with the delicious smell of frying bacon.

Dinah, in clean jodhpurs and a fresh white shirt and tie, paused a moment in the doorway, struck as she was every morning by how different everybody looked: you would never have believed that these smart young ladies and gentlemen, all in proper riding kit, could possibly be the same sloppy, ragged, smelly bunch of kids who had been toiling in the stables only a few minutes ago.

She poured a cup of tea and heaped a bowl with corn-flakes at the serving table and carried them to her place, looking up the length of the long table at the faces that had been so frighteningly strange three weeks ago, and were now so friendly and familiar. There were fourteen Horsemasters, divided into two groups to facilitate the division of stable duties. Blue Ride, on Dinah's side of the long table: Bee Bye next to her, and then Adrienne and Peanuts and Jill, with David and Roger beyond. And Mercy Hale all alone in state at the head of the table. And then the kids from Red Ride down the other side of the table: Ingrid Muus-Falck, the Norwegian girl, and Gretel Gotwals, the Dutch girl, and Toni Harper and Sally Burnham and Betsy Murphy and Lady Audrey Hughes, known as Speedy for the slow way she dragged herself around in the mornings, and the Italian boy, Vincenzo Lalli ...

'*Buon' giorno*, Dinah!' Enzo called, cheerfully, 'an' how is my American cousin this morning, eh?'

'Just fine, Spaghetti, just fine,' Dinah assured him and dug into her cornflakes hungrily, and tall blonde Ingrid said in her slow English:

'We are here truly a United of Nations, not? Tell me, Dinah, why do you come here so far, all the way from America? For Bee Bye, of course, I understand; she is very good rider and perhaps she must come so far to be perfect. But *you*, Dinah, you are not so – oh! I have been again stupid!'

David Perrin was whooping with laughter, and Ingrid's face turned scarlet; Dinah gave her a comforting wink and a grin and said cheerfully:

'I stink, huh? Well, I *do*, so you don't have to be embarrassed, Ingrid. Bee Bye's been riding all her life, and I'm kind of starting from scratch. But if I can get through this course and pass the Exams, I get to spend four years at the college I *want* to go to, instead of the State University which is what my father can afford. So ... here I am, kind of dumb but determined.'

She shrugged, stirring sugar into her tea, and David asked curiously:

'What college *do* you want to go to, Dinah? And what has this course got to do with it?'

'It's a small college,' Dinah explained, 'called Wells College. Small, and fashionable, and expensive. And good. Bee Bye's going there next fall, and we've always wanted to go together. Only – well, my father can't afford to send me there. But my grandmother left me a thousand dollars towards my education, and Bee Bye and I went and talked to the Dean, and the upshot of *that* was that the Dean finally said *if* I turn up in September with the Preliminary

Instructor's Certificate of the British Horse Society clutched in my hot little hand I can work my way through as Assistant Riding Mistress. And my father thought it over and *finally* said if I wanted to gamble my thousand dollars on a summer in England, it was all right with him so long as I get back in time to start *somewhere* at college in September.'

There was a moment of silence, and then David said quietly, 'Jolly good show! I hope you make it!' And Peanuts Pride called down the table, 'Luck, old girl!' And Jill Taylor, the plump Scots girl, lifted the lid off the platter of bacon and fried bread, and yelped as she always did:

'Anybody not want theirs?'

The clatter of breakfast resumed, and Dinah was grateful for a moment in which no one paid any attention to her. It *was* a gamble, and Dad hadn't really liked the idea much. And it *wasn't* as though the thousand dollars wouldn't really come out of Dad in the end if she should fail. True, it was Dinah's and Grandmother had left it to her; but it would have helped a lot to cover clothes and visits home and other incidentals during four years at State. Dinah hadn't thought of it that way at the time, and neither had Bee Bye; Dad must have, of course, but he'd never mentioned it...

It had been such a wonderful inspiration she and Bee Bye had had, and when the Dean had actually agreed to the idea, Dinah had been dazzled by a glittering daydream of returning from a glorious summer in Europe with Bee Bye to start at Wells. She had seen herself occasionally coming to class looking glamorous in boots and breeches, and gracefully vanishing afterwards to demonstrate the art of riding to an admiring group of pupils...

But it had been pretty darned thoughtless, because when you came right down to it Dad was taking all the risk. And what a risk it was! Most of these kids had been riding to hounds all their lives; they'd grown up with ponies and were familiar with horses and riding and stable work. And *they* all dreaded the British Horse Society Examinations at the end of the Horsemastership Course. So what chance did she really have?

'The List!' Bee Bye hissed excitedly and jostled Dinah's elbow, and all at once the babble of conversation hushed. Mercy Hale was standing at the head of the table, smart and crisp in her hacking jacket, and in her hand she held the List. And all heads were turned to Mercy.

'Tack up in twenty minutes, everybody,' Mercy announced unnecessarily, dropping her gaze to the List for a moment; she looked up again and said clearly, 'And here are the horses you will ride this morning: Miss Pride will ride Cornish Pasty –'

'Oh, my achin' back!' Peanuts groaned, and Dinah grinned at her maliciously. Corny never bucked, but he could pull like a train until your arms ached from holding him in, and what was worse he had a bone-shaking trot that simply jarred loose everything you had. One two-hour morning ride on Corny P. and you were guaranteed to be lame all day ...

In fact, Dinah thought, Corny P. was really a thoroughly good-for-nothing old horse; she could not understand why the School kept him. He was difficult to take care of and impossible to ride stylishly – whoever drew Corny P. for one of Captain Pinski's dressage lessons was in for a horrible morning, because *nobody* could collect the shambling old cob properly. Dinah felt a kind of grudging, exasperated affection for old Corny P., but she loathed taking care of him, and it did seem wasteful to lavish so much care and attention on such a valueless old horse. If only she could be assigned to groom, say, Nightingale.

'Mr Nicholson will ride Pipe Clay,' Mercy announced

primly, and Jill Taylor called out above the chorus of groans:

'Bags I the other end of the line from old Roger, then!' Jill Taylor yelped, and a chorus arose to echo her while Roger Nicholson looked thoroughly pleased. The huge white mare Pipe Clay was quarrelsome and would nip at any other horse or groom who unwarily came within reach of her great yellow teeth, but she was wonderful to ride, calm and steady and obedient, and with the smoothest possible gaits.

'Miss Wilcox,' Mercy called, and for a moment her cold blue eyes met Dinah's, and then looked down at the List again, 'will ride Blue Trout –'

'That's 10p!' Sally Burnham whooped derisively, and for a moment Dinah hated the big girl as the whole table roared with laughter, and she could only hope her own smile didn't look as sickly as it felt, 'Up the British Olympics; every horse in England can go in his private box, and Wilcox will pay the lot!'

In spite of the queasy tingling in her stomach Dinah had to laugh with the rest. As soon as she did, the scary feeling went away; you just couldn't feel scared when nobody else was, really. You had to put 10p in the fine box for the benefit of the British Olympic Equestrian Team every time you fell off a horse, and Dinah would almost certainly get a fall from Blue Trout this morning; she had never been able to hold the hard-mouthed little roan – he simply went faster and faster until he was completely out of control. But if the Major would just keep the class inside the covered school where there was soft sand and sawdust to fall on, she wouldn't get hurt . . .

'Mr Perrin will ride Claddagh Boy,' Mercy said, and a hush fell over the long table as all eyes turned to David, who shrugged and rolled his eyes heavenwards. Claddagh Boy was a new horse, a big young bay just bought from the

Irish National Stud; he was sometimes quiet and even lazy, but sometimes he bucked with a malevolent fury unequalled by any horse in Owen-Allerford's stables. Only David and Roger and Bee Bye and Ingrid, the four best riders, were ever assigned to Claddagh Boy, and he had already thrown Roger and Ingrid as well as Mercy Hale herself. Nobody jeered at David now, because the trial of Claddagh Boy against David Perrin was matching the School's most difficult horse against the Horsemasters' most skilled rider; the class sat in respectful silence.

'Miss Simms will ride Copper,' Mercy said coolly, and although the big sorrel was nearly as nappy as Claddagh Boy, Bee Bye simply nodded calmly as she caught Dinah's eye and rose from the table, pushing her chair back. Roger and David were leaving, too, going out through the open french windows on to the terrace to amble leisurely down towards the stables; Dinah and Bee Bye went out the other way, through the hall with its rack of riding mackintoshes and velvet caps and out of the front door to stand in the sunshine for a lazy minute before going down to saddle their horses. A car was just drawing away, rolling slowly up the climbing driveway in a small drift of reddish dust; Bee Bye murmured lazily:

'There go the Equitators, bless 'em. Have you seen this week's lot?'

'Uh-uh,' Dinah answered, shaking her head, 'but they can't be too good. Three days, and they're still on Trocadie and Kitty and the rest of the easy horses.'

Owen-Allerford taught not only the Horsemastership Course which took fifteen weeks and taught stable management and the rudiments of veterinary medicine as well as horsemanship to boys and girls preparing to ride for the British Horse Society Examinations in order to win the coveted Preliminary Instructor's Certificate; but also anyone of any age or degree of skill in riding who came to take private lessons or one-week courses in equitation or show-jumping or what was called combined training, meaning both equitation and cross-country jumping. These students were known as Equitators to distinguish them from the Horsemasters, with whom they were not encouraged to mingle; in the one-week courses they rode two hours every morning and an hour and a half every afternoon, but they did not do any work – they neither cared for horses nor cleaned tack. That was all done for them by the Horsemasters and by the working pupils at the School's Vale Stables, a mile and a half away, where fifteen more horses were kept.

The Equitators sometimes included some really fine riders, people who had ridden to hounds all winter over the most difficult country in England and came to Owen-Allerford at the end of the foxhunting season to correct the bad habits they had got into during the winter. And several members of the British Olympic Team had come, bringing their own horses for schooling over Owen-Allerford's formidable cross-country course. But quite frequently the Equitators were outright beginners, sometimes almost comically poor riders whose only experience had been docilely following one another behind an instructor in placid trots on London's Rotten Row; this week's group, whom Dinah hadn't seen, apparently fell into the latter category.

'You know,' Bee Bye murmured thoughtfully, 'I used to envy the Equitators, having nothing to do but ride and loaf around between times, no work to do ... but I don't think they have as much fun as we do, actually. Ever notice the humble way they look at our ragged lot whenever we pass 'em on the dead run to go muck out or clean tack or whatever? As though they were poor little amateurs looking up at a bunch of hard-boiled old professionals?'

The front door banged behind them, and Betsy Murphy said with feeling:

'*You* may think that all the fun's below the salt in this prison, Simms, but if I ever graduate *I* shall return as an Equitator. I shall lie late abed of a frosty mornin', and then I shall rise and descend to a leisurely breakfast, and saunter out of the stables where some poor ragged clot of an H.M. will be holdin' my horse for me, all saddled and bridled. I shall hand the poor shiverin' wretch my stick to hold, the while she gives me a leg up and adjusts my leathers for me, and I shall then nod graciously and canter off, knowing 'twill not be *me* cleans the tack or grooms the nag when I've had my morning's hack. Sure, and *that's* the fun in it, my lass!'

'For myself,' Adrienne put in sleepily, 'I shall not return to this place. Not as an Equitator, not as anything. For me, as soon as I reach home, I shall ask my father please to sell my horse; I do not wish ever to see a horse again. And for all the rest of my life I want only thing: I want not ever to leave my bed before it is time for lunch ... *Eh bien*, it is a lovely dream, that, but now I think we must hurry, no?'

'My word!' Betsy exclaimed, startled, 'we'd best run!'

And they were off, sprinting for the stables, the loose pebbles of the drive slipping and rolling beneath their jodhpur boots as they raced down the slight slope. Her elbows flapping to help her balance, Dinah tried to cling to her crop and her hard hat with one hand and button her hacking jacket with the other as she ran; it was no good, and she clattered over the bricks of the stable yard and into the tack-room and leaned against the wall, breathing hard from her run, and hurriedly buttoned the jacket there.

Setting down her hat and stick, she took Cornish Pasty's bridle from its rack and looped it over her arm; she dragged his saddle down and carried it at a smart lope across the stable yard to his stall. She hung the bridle on the end of the partition between his stall and the next and heaved the saddle deftly on to his back, placing it high on his withers and sliding it back an inch or two so that the hair beneath it would lie smooth. Kneeling on the straw, she reached under his belly to catch the dangling end of the cinch and draw it tight.

She got up quickly and turned to reach for the bridle, and saw that there were fresh droppings on the clean straw behind the horse; with a vexed exclamation she dived out of the stall to take the skip, a heavy iron dishpan, from its hook on the stable wall. Kneeling close behind Corny's heels, she carefully worked her hands under the straw and deftly flipped the droppings into the skip, and carried it out to empty it into the mucksack-draped wheelbarrow in the stable yard.

Returning, she picked up each of Corny P.'s hind feet in turn and inspected it; fortunately, he hadn't yet stepped in his droppings, his feet were clean. Relieved, Dinah caught up the bridle and went to his head. She unbuckled his stall collar and let it drop to the straw, drew his head down, and offered him the bit, spread across her left palm. The old horse nuzzled the steel snaffle with his soft lips but refused to open his mouth; deftly, Dinah slipped her thumb into the corner of his mouth and touched his tongue, and at once Corny opened his mouth and she slipped the bit into it. She dragged the bridle up over his ears and buckled the throat latch and then the dropped noseband, tugged at the bridle to settle it comfortably.

Ready! she thought, and let her pent-up breath out in a sigh of relief. Corny P. turned his head to regard her curiously, chewing lazily on his bit; impulsively Dinah put her arms round his neck and leaned against him again, closing her eyes and thinking dreamily that he *did* have so much personality. Even if he *was* a loathsome, untidy creature and a great, clumsy, heavy-footed fool to ride, he was really rather sweet when you got to know him ... It made her feel guilty that she wanted so much to be rid of him, to trade with one of the others; poor old Corny P., he had nobody to love him. But he certainly was an unlovable horse!

'File out, everybody!' Mercy Hale shrilled from the stable yard, and Dinah went to Corny's head, placing a hand on his chest and shoving. Corny took one slow careful step backwards and then another, feeling his way deliberately; Dinah backed him out and turned him and led him out of the stable. His hooves clopped loudly over the bricks of the stable yard, his head bobbed lazily up and down as he ambled along, his eyes half-closed. Ingrid was leading Cotton Socks out of Stable Two just ahead, and Dinah stopped, holding Corny P. to let Ingrid file out ahead; as she stood there Enzo Lalli emerged from Stable One leading Blue Trout, and suddenly began to gesticulate frantically at Dinah. She stared at the Italian boy, puzzled, as he pointed at her and then at Corny P. and then at the seat of his own well-tailored breeches; suddenly it dawned on her, and with a gasp of horror she dropped Corny's reins and dived back to grab his bandaged tail with both hands and yank, peeling the tail bandage off and stuffing it hastily into the front of her hacking jacket as she caught up his reins again and led him forward. There was a 2p fine for forgetting to take your tail bandage off before leaving the stable, but far worse than the small fine was the humiliation Mercy could heap upon your shrinking head ...

The horses and their grooms were bunched in the shade of the great trees overhanging the gravelled area outside the stable yard; as Dinah led Corny P. into the group, Peanuts ran up and took his reins from Dinah.

'Better take up those leathers,' Dinah suggested, 'I think they're long for you.'

'Righty-o,' Peanuts said, nodding, and Dinah turned away to look for Blue Trout. Dodging round Betsy Murphy and Night Life, and getting the black mare's tail swished across her face as she did so, she came up to Enzo and reached for the little roan's reins, murmuring:

'Thanks, Enzo. I *will* forget that flamin' bandage about every other morning!'

'*Prego, bella signorina!*' Enzo said with a sweeping bow, and flashed her his beautiful white smile and a melting look from liquid dark eyes before he spun away shouting, 'Mayfly! Where is the fortunate horse Mayfly? I, Enzo Lalli, will ride thees horse; w'ere is he?'

'That crazy Italian!' Bee Bye said, giggling. 'He can't ask a girl, *any* girl, to pass the cornflakes without making it a declaration of undying passion ... Where's Adrienne? She's supposed to ride my Booty, my beautiful horse, my lovely one, and here he is unclaimed. I have made his bed and fed him his breakfast and bathed him and brushed his teeth; I have plumped up his pillows and changed his pyjamas and dressed him in his best for the ungrateful girl, and where is she? Gone back to bed?'

'I am here,' Adrienne murmured and took Bootlegger's reins from Bee Bye, 'and I thank you, Bee Bye, for this so-pretty horse ... I have heard it said that *all* Italians are like our Enzo; do you believe this could be true?'

'If they are,' Bee Bye said blissfully, 'then I am going to visit Italy. For my ego, you understand. I –'

'All right, fall in!' Mercy called shrilly. 'Lead your horses down to the school and line up; check your girths and stirrup leathers, and mount when you are ready!'

Roger Nicholson, standing a little aside from the group and holding Pipe Clay by short reins, led the huge white mare slowly off towards the path that led down to the

Covered School, and the others waited to leave a respectful and cautious interval behind him before, one by one, they followed. Blue Trout threw his head up and hustled off in a brisk jog, crowding close against Shadow's quarters as he always liked to do, and Dinah, half-running to keep up, tried in vain to hold him back by dragging his head down. Blue Trout always crowded as close as he could get behind the horse in front of him; frequently enough he got kicked, but it never seemed to teach him any better . . .

They're all such *individuals*, Dinah thought, leading the tough little roan down the path towards the looming bulk of the Covered School while crickets chirped in the grass at her feet and birds sang in the trees overhead, just like people, there aren't any two horses alike.

The sun was warm on her shoulders now, and then she was in the shadow cast by the great weather-beaten building; she had one last glimpse of the green paddocks and the blue sea sparkling in the sunlight, and then they were in the cool dark cavernous interior of the school.

Chapter 3

The Covered School

The horses' hooves made no sound as they plodded round close to the slanted board walls; underfoot was a six-inch layer of soft sand mixed with sawdust, still showing the rippling comb-marks where it had been neatly raked level last night. But from time to time a stirrup iron scraped with a ringing, echoing sound against the boards; all along the walls all the way round the vast hall, at a height of about three feet, there ran a yellowish streak where the grey patina had been rubbed off the boards by the iron stirrups as the riders went round and round the school.

It was cool and dark in the school, the only light coming from a row of small windows high up overhead, and it smelled of damp sawdust and of aged wood and of horses, a good clean fragrance. High on the walls at each corner and in the middle of each side there were huge letters; at one end, also high up, was the visitors' gallery. Roger was leading Pipe Clay inwards from the wall now, just in front of the gallery; he halted the big mare there, and one by one the others turned in and halted in an even row.

Dinah turned Blue Trout in and halted him; she slipped her left arm through the reins and stepped back to run her hand under his belly, slipping two fingers between his belly and the girth. It was snug but not too tight; she would have to check it again after riding him for a few minutes, when he would be less swollen with air, but it did not need adjusting now.

The stirrup irons were run up properly tight against

the saddle; she pulled the near one down and measured the length of the leather, placing her knuckles against the bar at its top and the stirrup iron in her armpit. The leathers were too long, and she took each of them up two holes.

Blue Trout threw his head up suddenly and snorted, pawing the sawdust at his feet; Dinah said soothingly, 'Wuh-ho-o, Blue Trout; wuh-ho-o, boy; steady, old boy...'

She took up the reins snugly, holding them in her left hand on top of Blue Trout's withers, then she put her left foot into the near stirrup and took a firm hold on the back of the saddle with her right hand and swung smoothly up into the saddle, swinging her right leg high to clear his rump without kicking him. She felt for the off stirrup with her right foot and found it, and settled deep into the saddle, forcing her heels down as far as she could. She settled her velvet cap squarely on her head, and took up the reins in both hands, sitting erect in the saddle, ready. Along the long row the others were mounting now; then they were all mounted and sitting their horses quietly, except Adrienne, desperately hopping about on one foot, trying vainly to hoist herself aboard the towering Bootlegger while the big horse blandly stepped round in a circle each time she put her weight in the stirrup.

A suppressed ripple of laughter ran down the row, and then David Perrin vaulted lightly out of his saddle and tossed Claddagh Boy's reins to Roger Nicholson to hold. Interlacing his fingers, David placed his interlocked hands on his bent knee; Adrienne put her knee into them and David counted, 'One, two, three!' and lifted her neatly into Bootlegger's saddle. He ran back and reclaimed Claddagh Boy's reins from Roger and remounted himself; and Mercy Hale, standing at attention in the middle of the vast school, piped:

'Walk forward, everybody, and in the track ... left –
turn!'

Dinah put her heels firmly to Blue Trout's girth, and
the roan moved forward alertly at once; as he came up
against the long wall of the school and Dinah turned him
left in the track he was crowding close behind Copper's
quarters, as usual. And Copper was a nappy horse; it didn't
take much to make the big sorrel kick. Dinah took a firm
grip on the reins and hauled back with all her strength,
and was rewarded by seeing a clear foot of space grow between Blue Trout's nose and Copper's glistening quarters.
He would pull away again, she knew; he was stronger than
she, and he would have his way in the end ...

But now the tingling delight of riding was growing in
her as it always did; she could feel the warmth of the horse
beneath her and the enormous power of the living body
moving docilely along, carrying her; she could see the
rippling muscles in his shoulders and feel the surge of
strength in his mighty quarters and the rhythmic swell of
his ribs as he breathed. Blue Trout's head bobbed up and
down as he walked, leaning forward eagerly into his bit;
between his alert erect forward-pointing ears she could see
the hard ropes of muscle moving under the shining cop-
pery quarters of the horse ahead.

'Space out, everybody!' Mercy Hale was shrieking.
'*Space* out; keep one horse's length apart! Dinah Wilcox,
don't let Blue Trout crowd Copper that way; d'you want
to get kicked? Roger, you're cutting off corners; keep Pipe
Clay in the track, please! Adrienne, *ride* Bootlegger up
into the corners; you know he'll go where he pleases if you
haven't any more contact than that! Jill, keep your heels
down, please; you're –'

The school door slid open and closed again, and Mercy's
voice cut off abruptly, as Major Brooke strode briskly to
the middle of the school. He spoke briefly in an undertone

to Mercy, listened to her reply, and nodded curtly in dismissal, preparing to take over the class. Mercy trotted out, and the Major stood slender and spruce and erect in the middle of the school, tapping gleaming boots with a swagger stick as he surveyed with frosty blue eyes the circling string of horses and riders. And then the Major's white teeth flashed in his lean ruddy face, and he snapped crisply:

'Class, prepare to trot ... T-r-r-rot-t!'

Blue Trout knew the Major's voice; he also knew the meaning of the word *trot*. He did not wait for Dinah's heels against his girth to urge him on; instead, he plunged forward eagerly, and rammed his hard blue nose into Copper's gleaming muscular rump. Copper promptly lashed out with both hind legs in a vicious kick, narrowly missing Blue Trout and making the school ring with the echoing slam of his hooves against the boards; Blue Trout threw his head up, snorting, and dodged out of line and into the raked expanse of sawdust in the middle of the school.

'In the centre, Miss Wilcox!' the Major commanded, and added with an ironic grin, 'Ah, I see you are in the centre already! Very commendable – but neither you nor your horse is to anticipate commands in the future! Ride him over to me, please.'

Flaming with embarrassment, Dinah rode miserably into the centre of the school, aware of the rest of the class continuing decorously round and round without looking at her as Blue Trout halted abruptly in front of Major Brooke. The Major took one step forward and took hold of the reins quite close to Blue Trout's bit; he said crisply, in his clipped impersonal voice:

'Your horse will not pay attention to someone else's commands, Miss Wilcox, if he is paying attention to you. Therefore you must command his attention, by proper application of the aids. You have *no* contact with Blue

Trout's mouth at the moment, Miss Wilcox; that is why
he is paying no attention to you, and why he listened instead to me and responded to my command. Please lift
your hands and hold your reins firmly –'

Dinah did as she was told, and felt a very gentle but still
firm and steady tugging at her hands as the Major drew
the reins taut with his own.

'If you will try to maintain precisely this much contact
with your horse's mouth at all times, Miss Wilcox,' the
Major said incisively, 'you will find it much easier to
communicate your commands to him. All right – join the
ride!'

'Yes, sir,' Dinah murmured meekly. She took up on her
left rein and put her heels into Blue Trout's sides, and the
little roan swung left and broke into a trot immediately,
crowding into line just in front of Pipe Clay – the
last place in the world Dinah wanted to be. But the Major
was probably watching her; there was nothing for it but to
pretend Blue Trout had responded smartly to her command. Bending slightly forward, she rose a little in her
stirrups to ease the jar of the one-two beat of Blue Trout's
trot; remembering to keep an eye on his outside shoulder
and return to her saddle each time it moved back, she rose
and fell rhythmically, rose and fell, rose and fell …
Adrienne was ahead of her now, on Bootlegger; Adrienne
was posting to the wrong shoulder, and as Dinah observed
this, Adrienne did too and sat down hard for one bumping
step and rose again, this time correctly. There was a little
dust in the air now, and she was beginning to feel quite
warm; there was a trace of dampness on Blue Trout's neck.
The school was full of muted sound: the creak of saddles
and the muffled thudding of the horses' hooves at a fast
trot on the sawdust, and occasionally the ringing scrape of
a stirrup along the boards …

'Keep the heel *down*, Miss Wilcox!' the Major called

clearly, and guiltily Dinah realized that as she rose in her stirrups her toes were indeed slipping to point comfortably downwards, and her heels came up. She stretched her Achilles tendons agonizingly, straining to force her heels down; the Major called out loudly:

'Leading file ... at the K marker ... change ... the rein!'

Bee Bye Simms on Copper, three horses ahead, rounded the corner of the school and turned smartly in at the K marker to ride diagonally across the school, sitting down for one step as she made her inward turn and rising again to what would be Copper's outside shoulder trotting round in the opposite direction. Peanuts Pride, on Cornish Pasty, followed Bee Bye precisely. And then came Adrienne on Bootlegger, and to Dinah's horror as she prepared to follow Adrienne into the turn Adrienne did not turn at all, but continued serenely trotting round the school in the original direction.

Dinah hauled Blue Trout round with an effort to follow Bee Bye and Peanuts; she sensed Roger and Pipe Clay following her, and from the muffled snickers far behind her knew that all the others were executing the manoeuvre correctly, though she dared not look back. But she didn't have to look back; the Major's purpling face was quite enough ... poor Adrienne!

'Class ... *halt!*' the Major roared, and Dinah hauled back on her reins, but Blue Trout would not stop until he was nuzzling Corny P.'s rump, as usual. Dinah could look round now, and she did; the line was strung out raggedly round the school, but it was still a line. Except for Bee Bye, in the lead, who was face to face with an appalled-looking Adrienne, who was of course headed in the opposite direction and had halted just in time to avoid a head-on collision.

'Oh, *je m'excuse!*' Adrienne cried, turning to direct a blinding blue gaze of contrition at the Major's scarlet countenance. '*Je suis désolée; je n'ai pas compris* – I am veree sorree, Major Brooke; once again I 'ave fail to comprehend . . . You will forgive?'

Silence descended over the school as the Horsemasters held their collective breath. The Major regained his self-control with a visible effort; he did not, to everyone's disappointment, throw his jaunty little green hat to the sawdust and stamp on it as he had occasionally been known to do when driven beyond human endurance by the ineptitude of the class. He nodded rather curtly to Adrienne, and raised his voice to command the class at large.

'Check your cinches at the halt, and prepare to canter *from* the halt. I do *not* want to see *anyone* trotting after the command to canter is given . . . Perhaps, Miss deMarigny, if you will ride Bootlegger into file behind Mr Perrin on Claddagh Boy, and when in doubt do as Mr Perrin does, we shall have fewer misunderstandings . . .'

Dinah had bent forward and reached down to slip her hand between Blue Trout's girth and his body; the girth was good and loose. She straightened up in the saddle and stuck her left leg straight out in front of her, feeling under the saddle flap with her left hand for the straps to cinch it up tight. She found one and yanked it up two holes, then the other . . . that ought to do it.

'Take up your reins,' the Major ordered, and all over the school saddles creaked as the riders collected themselves and their horses. 'Prepare, from the halt, to canter. From the halt . . . Can-n-*ter-r-r*!'

Dinah had taken up her reins to the same firm, gentle contact the Major had demonstrated; Blue Trout's ears had come up, alert and attentive. At the command *prepare* she had added a delicate trace of extra tension to the inside rein; when the Major called 'Can-ter!' she kept her inside leg firmly on the girth and moved her outside leg away from Blue Trout's body and swung it back to apply it firmly behind the girth. Blue Trout gathered himself and sprang forward, launching into a rocking canter immediately, and Dinah thought in giddy elation *Perfect! I did it perfectly*, and I've never come close to cantering from the halt before; oh, I *do* hope the Major was watching.

She kept her inside leg on the girth to encourage the roan on and let her upper body sway a little with the rhythm of his canter, bringing her weight a little to the inside on the corners with her inside shoulder forward. But if the Major had been watching, he said nothing about it; he said nothing to anyone as the circle of riders raced round and round in the suddenly confined space of the Covered School, frighteningly close to one another at this increased pace. And now the thudding of hooves in the sawdust track was audible – still muffled, but unmistakably the sound of a thundering herd of horses running together, kicking up dark-brown clods ... And now the Major, having seen enough and looking grim and unforgiving, began to shout at them as they rode:

'Lower your heels, Miss Harper, *get those heels down*! You cannot maintain your seat, nor your impulsion, if your toes are pointing down and your heels up! ... Mr Lalli, Mayfly is *trotting*; are you unable, Mr Lalli, to distinguish between a trot and a canter? ... Miss deMarigny, you have no contact with that horse's mouth at *all, no* contact, *no contact*! You are not riding Bootlegger at all; he is simply following the horse ahead of him! And you are just sitting up there on his back, a slave to his every whim! Oh, my word! ... Miss Murphy, your horse is contra-cantering, he is cantering on the wrong lead; can't you *feel* how wrong it is?' The Major's voice rose to a tortured scream. He roared at Betsy, '*Miss Murphy!* Pull your horse down to a trot, and strike off again on the correct lead! Oh, my *word*!'

Golly, Dinah thought, we aren't doing so well today, any of us! And the Major looks furious. I just hope *I* don't do anything more wrong!

She was beginning to tire now; grimly, she forced herself to concentrate. Keep that rein contact with Blue Trout's mouth, just this much; keep those heels *down*; ride erect, with back slightly hollowed. Keep hands low. Don't let him cut off the corners; ride him right up into 'em ...

'At the H Marker,' the Major shouted, 'with Mr Perrin as the leading file ... a simple change of lead!'

Dinah saw David ride round the corner, with Adrienne close on his heels; she saw him pull Claddagh Boy down to a trot as he turned to cross the school on a diagonal line, and then to one step at a walk in the middle of the school and into a trot again. She saw Adrienne, following, emulate David's splendid example perfectly, and shifted her gaze back to David to watch with admiration as he completed the manoeuvre.

But he didn't complete it. Just at the point where the big bay gelding came out of the diagonal and into the track again, at the moment when David tried to spur him into a canter on the opposite lead, Claddagh Boy suddenly humped his back and got his head down between his front feet and exploded into a fury of bucking, twisting and pitching and kicking while David, his face a white mask of concentration, fought with all the skill at his command to stay in the saddle and regain control of the big horse.

'Entire class *halt*!' the Major bellowed; unnecessarily, for they had all pulled their horses down from the canter to a ragged halt, craning to see as much as possible and still keep out of the way as much as possible. The Major's lean ruddy face was a study in excitement and delight as he watched the slim boy on the enraged bay horse; the same avid glitter was in all the other eyes, and Dinah knew it must be in her own, too, that tense *wanting* and *dreading* all at the same time ... she honestly did not know whether she hoped David would not be thrown, at last, or whether she hoped that this time he would ...

And then all of a sudden it was over and David had not come off; Claddagh Boy's head came up abruptly and he pranced a little, shying into the centre of the School and snorting, and then he steadied down submissively. And David, the ham, swept his hard hat off his head and made a sweeping bow to the school at large.

'An excellent performance, Mr Perrin,' the Major said dryly, while a subdued cheer arose from the Horsemasters. 'I'm sure we should all appreciate an encore, if you would care to oblige? No? Well, then, while Mr Perrin catches his breath and we are all at ease, I shall seize the opportunity to make a brief announcement of interest, I trust, to you all ...'

The Major coughed and glanced about, tapping his gleaming boot with his stick, to make sure he had everyone's attention. He had. He said crisply:

'On the Friday preceding your examinations at the end of this course, the South Dorset Hunt will conduct Hunter Trials near Dorchester, some seventy miles from here. There will be no classes on that day, and those of you who feel it wise to spend what free time you have in studying will, of course, be free to do so. However, the School has entered three horses in these Trials – Bay Rum, Pennant, and Mayfly – in the hope that they may make a sufficiently good showing to be sold at an advantageous price. Captain Pinski will ride Bay Rum, Mercy Hale will ride Pennant, and I shall ride Mayfly myself. Now, am I correct in assuming that in spite of the nearness of the B.H.S. Examinations some of you *might* think it educational if you were permitted to take the day off from school and watch our horses in competition?'

The shriek that went up was one of sheer delirium; it rattled the rafters of the Covered School, and it was followed by a babble of eager voices, not one of which could be heard clearly. The Major waited a dramatic moment, his frosty blue eyes sparkling with pleasure; he raised an imperious hand, and instantly a hush fell over the school.

'You cannot all go, of course,' he said decisively, 'at least half of you must remain here to look after the horses that stay behind. But if you can make independent arrangements for transportation, the other half may go. Now, you have already been divided into two groups to facilitate the division of stable duties and half-holidays and free weekends; we shall therefore, to be fair, institute a merit system, from today, to determine whether Red Ride or Blue Ride is to be rewarded with the day free to attend the Trials. Mercy Hale will inspect your horses, your stables, your tack, and your personal attire periodically and assign demerits for any impropriety; the Ride accumulating fewer demerits before the Trials will be free to attend if they so desire ...'

He paused, and there was not one sound from the class; he dropped his voice to a conversational level and added quietly:

'I should like to urge you all to pay more careful attention to your riding kit in particular. We do *not*, at this School, turn out to ride in a pullover nor in a blouse or in any kit other than a *clean* shirt with collar and tie, worn properly with a hacking jacket, hard hat, and jodhpurs or boots and breeches. Very well, let us get on with the lesson. Prepare to walk ... Walk, *march*!'

Back in the stables. Dinah raced through quarter-grooming Corny P., going over him rapidly and hard with the dandy brush, picking out his feet and putting his tail bandage back on as she did after every morning's ride. Then she got him a bucket of fresh water and raced for the tack-room, where most of the others were already assembled and hard at work. There was no free hook from which to hang Corny's bridle while cleaning it, so Dinah hung it on its rack temporarily, hoisted his saddle on to a sawhorse and began sponging it down with a soft cloth wrung out in warm water, preparatory to saddle-soaping it thoroughly.

'We've just *got* to do it, Red Ride!' Toni Harper breathed prayerfully, her eyes half-closed and dreaming. 'To watch Captain Pinski ride in a Trial! *And* the Major! And maybe even to see Mercy get thrown, I hope! Oh, I'd give *anything* to go!'

'Well, you won't, y'know,' Peanuts Pride told her, grinning from behind the tangle of the bridle she was cleaning. 'Blue Ride'll go. Class will tell, and we've got it, girl. Only thing in the world we have to worry about is getting Adrienne out of bed in the morning; aside from that it's a cinch for us!'

'For this,' Adrienne murmured solemnly, 'I think I will get up in the morning, even. Do you think perhaps Mercy will really get hurt?'

'She could, y'know,' David put in. 'Mercy isn't really good enough for this sort of thing, and she hasn't the strength to hold Pennant over a hard cross-country course. It's a far cry from show-jumping, that. They'll probably go off in pairs, just flat out over all kinds of fences and ditches and banks, and Pennant is going to run with the other horse; Mercy'll never hold her. And running out of control over a Hunter Trial course is no sport for those of faint heart or fragile bones!'

The tack-room was silent for a moment, in deference to David's expert opinion, and Dinah shivered a little. She loathed Mercy Hale; she had never in her life detested anyone as she did the small fair-haired martinet who seemed to relish pulling her rank, making things as difficult as she could for the others, being petty and spiteful and mean. And still it seemed a little strong to talk so cheerfully about Mercy getting hurt, maybe even *killed*, especially if there was any chance that she seriously might. ... Had David been serious? Yes, she thought, he had ...

'Killing's too good for Mercy,' Jill Taylor cried from the bench beneath the window, and pointed excitedly with a can of brass polish. 'Have you seen the demerit list? My *word*, but isn't she going to enjoy handing those out! Oh, my aching back!'

Dinah dropped her washcloth and joined the rush to where Jill stood; craning, she could read the list in Mercy's careful handwriting:

DEMERITS

Dirty stable or manger	5
Dirty tack	5
Untidy or improper riding kit . .	3
Tail bandage left on	1
Late to stables	2
Extra duties not performed . . .	5
Dirt on horse	5
Feet not picked out	5
Insufficient bedding	3

The list went on and on, but Dinah could not see the bottom part of the sheet over the heads in front of her; she went back disconsolately to her half-cleaned saddle. And gradually the group at the bench broke up and returned to their tasks; it was a long, silent, thoughtful moment before plump Jill spoke again, her voice hard:

'She'll really *enjoy* handing out those demerits, the nasty little sadist,' Jill said decisively, and in silence all the others agreed with her. 'That's what I mind. It's not the demerits, it's Mercy Hale. There isn't one thing wrong with that girl that wouldn't be instantly remedied if she *did* get herself killed trying to ride Pennant at the Trials!'

And then Mercy's thin voice cut in sharply:

'All right, everybody! Finish your tack and get on the yards, please! And Adrienne, your horse's feet haven't been picked out; I'm giving Blue Ride five demerits. Please go and pick his feet out now.'

In the shocked, shamed hush no one raised a voice to comment or protest, but Mercy gave no sign of having heard Jill's outburst, although she *must* have heard it. She stood straight and slight in the doorway for a moment, moving a little aside as Adrienne went silently out, and surveyed them all without warmth. And then she turned and was gone.

'Oh, *golly*!' Jill wailed in distress, 'I didn't know she was in there! I didn't *know*!'

'Sure, an' if it's worryin' about hurting her feelings you are,' Betsy crooned, and put a consoling arm over Jill's plump shoulders, 'you need not, for I'm sure the girl has no feelings to be hurt!'

'Hurt her *feelings*!' Jill echoed scornfully. 'My hoof! What worries *me* is, she'll demerit me to death for this! Yipe – we better get on those yards! What's the Demerit List say, Late to stables, two points?'

Chapter 4

Two Armed Camps

Mercy Hale did nothing, in the days that followed, to lessen the deep antipathy all the Horsemasters felt for her; she seemed to redouble her efforts to persecute them all relentlessly and with cold relish, almost as though she *wanted* them all to hate her. Bleak and unfriendly and aloof, she seemed to be everywhere at once; nothing escaped her inspections, and she handed out demerits with merciless vindictive pleasure.

She found the tiniest possible speck of dried saliva inside the interlocked joints of Bootlegger's snaffle bit, and Blue Ride got five demerits for dirty tack; Bee Bye, furious, thereupon took to visiting the tack-room in the evenings after dinner, dismantling Bootlegger's bridle completely and polishing not only the bit but even the tongues of the tiniest buckles with a pipe cleaner after she had thoroughly cleaned everything else in the normal fashion.

Enzo Lalli, determined to set a good example for Red Ride, went without the tea for which the ever-hungry, ever-tired Horsemasters were grateful every afternoon, to spend that cherished three-quarters of an hour spring-cleaning Blue Trout's stall. He led the little roan outside and tied him while he carried out all the straw in his stall, scrubbed the concrete floor beneath and the board sides and the manger, and then bedded Blue Trout down in an absolutely immaculate stall. And ten minutes later Mercy found exactly three dried-up old oats stuck under the lip of the manger, and gave Red Ride five demerits.

Nor did the Head Girl confine herself to being in the

places her job would normally be expected to require of her, nor to normal working hours. She caught poor Adrienne, five minutes after having been mendaciously assured by three members of Blue Ride that Adrienne *was* mucking out Nutmeg and must have just stepped out for something a minute ago, by suddenly racing up to Allerford House and slamming into Adrienne's room, where Adrienne was just dragging herself out of bed. Two demerits, Blue Ride. And that seemed to give Mercy a malevolent idea: every morning from then on, when she banged on the feed bin and called 'Yards, everybody; yards, please!' the last Horsemaster to stop strapping his horse and dash out to sweep the stable yard automatically got two demerits. It made for some wild scrambles and jostling, and inevitably a certain amount of bad feeling grew between the members of the two Rides.

Prior to the Major's announcement of the Horse Trials and the institution of the demerit system, the three boys and eleven girls had all got along quite well together. They had been strange to one another at first, and excessively polite until the strangeness wore off; and then the politeness had been replaced by the friendly rudeness of familiarity. But everyone had liked everyone else, or at least no one had *disliked* anyone else very strongly. If you'd cleaned your bridle and still had a few minutes to spare, instead of leaving the tack-room you'd be quite likely to pitch in and help someone else – *anyone* else – clean hers. Everyone had too much work to do; you helped out wherever you could.

The Merit System changed that; it set up a competition that rapidly divided the Horsemasters into two armed camps, and built up a growing hostility between Blue Ride and Red Ride. David finished cleaning his tack one afternoon and promptly pitched in to help finish Jill's; and then Bee Bye finished hers and looked around for someone to help, and saw that Betsy and Gretel, who had been polishing brasses, each had a whole bridle to do. But Betsy and Gretel were on Red Ride, and after a moment's hesitation Bee Bye turned and left the tack-room.

Even Enzo Lalli, having finished bedding down Blue Trout and finding himself with three-quarters of a bale of clean new straw left over, started to offer it with a gallant flourish to Sally Burnham, who was just leaving the next stall to carry down a bale for Nightingale. But Sally was on Blue Ride, and Enzo checked himself with an effort; dolorously, he spread the unneeded extra straw about Blue Trout's stall.

It got so that each Ride was a solid, fiercely loyal bloc dedicated to helping one another in any way possible, and not above hindering the opposing faction, whose members were to be treated with formal politeness but no real cordiality. And then, just to mix things up further, Mercy switched Sally Burnham from Blue Ride to Red Ride, and Jill Taylor from Red Ride to Blue; and in two days Sally was no longer Dinah's ally but her enemy, and Jill no longer her enemy but a fast friend and ally ...

But one thing the warring factions agreed upon: they were unanimous in their bitter enmity for Mercy Hale.

'The girl's not *normal*!' Bee Bye cried in the course of a Blue Room bull session at bedtime and lowered her voice to a dramatic whisper, and they all bent forward avidly as she said, 'She doesn't go to bed, she just sneaks around all night! I was down in the tack-room last night, late – it must have been nine-thirty. And just as I was hanging up my bridle in *she* came without a sound, and without saying a single word to me she started going from rack to rack inspecting every bridle and saddle in the place! And, I mean, inspecting 'em *thoroughly*! At nine-thirty at night!'

Such behaviour was definitely not normal, they all agreed; it was spiteful and vindictive and petty. No getting round it, Mercy enjoyed handing out demerits; enjoyed it so much she'd rather spend her spare time looking for tiny little things to find fault with than do anything else. And this in spite of the fact that, as everyone knew, Mercy got up a full hour earlier than the Horsemasters every morning, to go out at five-thirty and hack her beloved Pennant up over the Downs for an hour before the day's work began ...

So, fused into two solid blocs by the ferocity of their competition and further driven by their resentment of Mercy, the Horsemasters drove themselves to work harder than ever before. The stables were cleaner and the horses better groomed and strapped than ever before, and in less time; it did absolutely no good to save time, however, because if you finished what you were supposed to be doing ahead of time, Mercy would turn up immediately and assign you some extra chore. Still, you couldn't work more slowly or less hard than your team-mates; so long as they were doing their absolute best, you couldn't very well do anything less than your own.

The daily routine at Owen-Allerford gradually became the pattern of Dinah's life until she felt as though she had never known any other. Up at quarter past six to attend to stable duties; then the morning riding lesson with the Major on Mondays and Tuesdays and Thursdays, and with Captain Pinski on Wednesdays and Fridays. Then after lunch a half-hour free to finish cleaning tack, and then an hour and a half's lecture on veterinary medicine or horse training or stable management from Mr Ffolliott. And then bed down Corny P. and water him and sweep the yards once more before tea, and feed him; then after tea go down and skip out his stall and put on his rug and give him his hay net. And then, unless it was her week for late watering at eight o'clock, she was finished for the day.

Thursdays were half-holidays for one Ride each week,

and the other Ride was free from lunch time Saturday until Monday morning. Saturday mornings, instead of riding classes, all the Horsemasters were taken on a two-hour hack over the Downs; whichever Ride had the weekend off was free as soon as they had returned from the hack, quartered their horses, and cleaned their tack.

As the routine grew more familiar and Dinah herself more skilful at her work she began to love the life at School, although whenever she thought of the B.H.S. Examinations to come at the end of the course she got a cold knot of apprehension in her stomach. Even if she could learn to ride well enough to pass that part of the Exam, she would still have to pass both an oral and a written examination on Stable Management and Minor Ailments and General Knowledge, all of which Mr Ffolliott was doing his best every afternoon to cram into the heads of the Horsemasters. But as they sprawled informally about the Blue Room assiduously taking notes, some of them on chairs and couches and others on the floor, Dinah found her notes becoming more and more bewildering; she was sure she would never manage to remember it all.

'Colic,' Mr Ffolliott pronounced firmly, and peered over the tops of his spectacles owlishly and repeated, 'colic. That's a heading. Write it down. Colic is a bellyache. Don't write that down. Doesn't sound dignified. But that's what it is. Causes: unsuitable food – that could be mouldy hay; or too much boiled grain or too much green food or new oats; or sudden change of food; or watering and working too soon after feeding; or worms; or chills; or crib-biting or wind-sucking; or bolting food. Symptoms – well, there's two kind of colic, got different symptoms. To begin with –'

'*Wait!*' Ingrid cried desperately, scribbling in her note-book, 'I have not yet written –'

Mr Ffolliott sighed, and waited; he continued, droning, '*Spasmodic colic*. Pain not continuous, intervals of ease. Horse kicks at its belly, paws ground, stamps, lies down and tries to roll, looks down at its sides, sweats in patches. *Flatulent colic*. This is due to fermentation of food and formation of gases in the bowels. The belly is inflated, pain is continuous but not so severe as in spasmodic colic. Horse appears uneasy, wanders around in his box as if wanting to lie down but afraid to do so . . .'

Dinah scrawled frantically in her notebook; she had filled one book entirely and was working on her second, and the course was only in its sixth week. Nine more weeks, she calculated, and she would have at least three notebooks full of symptoms and treatments and outlandish names of ailments that could beset a horse all too frequently; how could she possibly familiarize herself with enough of them to pass the examination?

'Treatment,' Mr Ffolliott droned, and consulted his own notes. 'If outside, get horse to nearest box and encourage him to stale. Throw straw against his belly and whistle, that'll help. Keep him warm. Walking exercise may help. Give him a colic drench. Hot blankets rolled up and applied to belly will relieve pain and stimulate action of the bowels. If the pain is not relieved within one hour, send for the vet.'

Jill Taylor, sprawled on the floor before the electric fire which wasn't really needed on this warm afternoon, was writing notes with one hand; with the other she was toasting a slice of bread on a fork before the glowing coils. She muttered,

'*I'd 've* sent for the flaming vet the minute old Shadow started groaning!'

'What's a colic drench, Mr Ffolliott?' Dinah asked, and the wiry old man scratched his head and peered at her over his spectacles.

'Could be any one of a lot of 'em, Dinah,' he answered. 'Every vet's got his favourite; you want to keep *your* vet's favourite on hand all the time. Then if it doesn't work it's *his* fault, not yours. *I* use two tablespoonfuls of turpentine, two tablespoonfuls of whisky, and a pint of linseed oil. Warm. But that's only what I use.'

Dinah wrote it down, nevertheless; Mr Ffolliott had been breeding, training, and dealing in horses for fifty years or more, and his recipe ought to be worthwhile, she felt.

'All right,' Mr Ffolliott said, 'that's about enough of the minor ailments for today; don't want to give you more at one time than you can keep straight in your minds. We've got another half-hour. Let's go on to the teeth. How many of you can age a horse by his teeth?'

Bee Bye's hand went up at once, and David's, and Ingrid's, and Gretel's; after a moment Roger Nicholson raised his half-way, hesitantly, and Mr Ffolliott gave him a swift grin, his sharp eyes twinkling behind the spectacles.

'Only farmer in the place,' Mr Ffolliott said cheerfully, 'and *he's* the doubtful one. How so, Roger?'

Roger blushed furiously; he mumbled, embarrassed, 'Well . . . it isn't absolutely certain, y'know . . . if I know how the horse has been fed, and know nobody's tampered with his mouth to make him look younger, I can give a pretty good guess at his age up to nine years. But if I were buying a horse from a strange dealer, I'd bear in mind that I was only guessing, *especially* if I thought the horse was somewhere over nine years old.'

'Couldn't do better m'self, y'know,' Mr Ffolliott said cheerfully, 'so suppose you tell us all what *you'd* look for. You just go right ahead; I'm tired of talking anyway . . .'

But Dinah could not make sense of Roger's halting discourse on the various ages at which certain of a horse's teeth appeared and at which they later came into wear;

she had never really looked at Corny P.'s teeth carefully, and all she could visualize effectively was that a horse has six biting teeth in the front of his mouth and then a smooth gap of gum for several inches between those and the chewing teeth at the back. She had already learned that it was entirely safe to put her thumb in the corner of Corny's mouth to make him open it for the bit, but the rest of this discussion was beyond her. She looked at her senseless notes and gave up in despair, promising herself that she would get Roger to show her, in the stable, what to look for.

So, while Roger stammered on, she leafed back through the pages of her notebook unhappily, reading her notes on such ailments as laminitis and ringbone and bog spavins and thoroughpin and lampas and curb and splints and navicular disease, and feeling increasingly certain that she would *never* be able to remember one from another. She couldn't even remember what they *were*, let alone glibly recite the symptoms, causes, and treatment for each – how would she *ever* get ready for the Exam? It was impossible!

But most of the others seemed to take these Blue Room lectures in their stride every afternoon; quite a few of them seemed to nod understandingly as though what Mr Ffolliott had to say simply confirmed what they had been told before. They've all had so much *experience*! Dinah thought desperately; how can I ever catch up?

It was drizzling miserably on the Thursday of Blue Ride's half-holiday; the skies were leaden grey and the ground underfoot was sodden, the gravel driveway covered with a slippery film of reddish mud. Blue Ride finished lunch and returned to the tack-room to finish cleaning tack; they were then free for the rest of the day, since there was no lecture on Thursday afternoon and Red Ride was assigned to take care of all the horses for the rest of the day. But they hung around indecisively on this Thursday, suspiciously watching whenever a Red Rider performed any routine service for a Blue Rider horse; their carefree attitude was gone, and it was not only the miserable weather that made them all reluctant to leave the stables, even though they had changed into casual clothes to visit the village of Owen. The rivalry that had split the class had now grown so intense that each of them jealously begrudged a member of the other Ride even the privilege of doing her stable work.

Dinah had spent a solid twenty minutes polishing Corny P.'s stirrups and replacing them on his saddle; when she could find absolutely nothing else to do in the tackroom she wandered morosely out to join David and Peanuts and Jill, and the four of them stood in the doorway of Stable Three taking shelter from the drizzle and feeling foolishly out of place in their clean town clothes while the stable-clad tatterdemalions of Red Ride bustled busily back and forth. And then Bee Bye, in a cashmere sweater and tweed skirt and medium heels and lipstick, suddenly emerged from Stable One carefully carrying a skip, and as she briskly dumped her load of Bootlegger's droppings into the barrow they all exploded into hysterical laughter.

'All right!' Bee Bye said, scowling and then joining in, 'that does it! Rain or no rain, let's walk to the village! We can at least go to visit the Vale stables and see some new faces, horses, *and* people. And I guess I don't *really* suspect even that murderous Betsy Murphy of neglecting my fair Booty on my afternoon off!'

Betsy, passing, made a rude sound with her lips; Jill yelped:

'And we can have tea in the village! A real cream tea, with lashings of clotted cream and jam and – Ready, I!'

So they went, all of them but Adrienne, who had taken a bath and was luxuriating in bed with a stack of maga-

zines and a box of bon-bons. With riding mackintoshes
turned up over their ears and their hands shoved deep
into pockets, they strode briskly along the wet-glistening
narrow road with its hedge-topped grassy banks rising
steep on either side, giggling for no reason at all while
sparkling droplets of moisture gathered in their hair and
glistened on their faces. To Dinah, the thatched roofs of
the little cottages along the way, and the few absurdly old-
fashioned little cars that passed them, and the impossible
neatness of the fields and hedgerows were all like something out of a story book; the entire English countryside
was a tidy and exquisite miniature. And the fresh English
voices all around her, bubbling with enthusiasm but still
always so delightfully polite in a well-trained matter-of-
fact way, as nobody was ever polite at home, not kids to
each other anyway ... She and Bee Bye had remarked on
it before; everybody in England seemed to have good
manners without ever thinking about it.

'I say, Dynamite!' David fell into step with her, 'why so
very pensive? Everyone else is talking nineteen to the
dozen, and you've said not one murmur since we left.
Cold? Wet? Want to turn back?'

'I was thinking,' Dinah said lazily, and suddenly realized that Bee Bye and Peanuts and Roger and Jill were
listening curiously too, and that she did not want to blurt
out what she had been thinking about to all of them as she
had been about to do, without thinking, to David. 'I was
thinking,' she repeated, 'that of all of us on the whole
course, you and Bee Bye are the only ones who haven't
had a fall yet. And I was wondering which of you would be
the first to pay up your 10p. Or if maybe you'll both get
through without having a fall at all?'

'Not likely!' David said, laughing. 'As I understand it
nobody's *ever* got through the H.M. Course at Owen-
Allerford without at least one fall; it's rather a tradition,

you know. And there've been some jolly good horsemen here; I rather think that if one doesn't come unstuck in the natural order of things the Major must make a special effort to get one off. Corn the horse well and give him a day's rest, then shove a burr under his saddle and send you off round the cross-country course; that sort of thing. Can't let the old School down, y'know; tradition and all that . . . So I dare say our time will come, what, Bee Bye?'

'Speak for yourself!' Bee Bye answered rudely. 'They're *your* silly traditions, not mine!'

'*Bee Bye Simms!*' Dinah gasped, shocked and ashamed for her friend; but Bee Bye would not look at Dinah. She simply strode on looking sullenly straight ahead, her face dark and defiant. Her long-smouldering antipathy to David was out in the open now; from Bee Bye's expression she was not sorry for it.

The others seemed quite accidentally to have drifted a few steps away, to be quite oblivious. Roger was pointing out some invisible bird in a nearby field to Peanuts; Jill was absorbedly kicking a pebble ahead of her, head down.

'In that case,' David said pleasantly, smiling but looking a little white round the mouth, 'I think I must remember to invoke another honoured tradition. *Ladies first!*'

He nodded graciously, still smiling, and lengthened his stride, his long legs carrying him rapidly away from them all towards the village. And behind him he left an acutely uncomfortable silence, and five people who unhappily did not want to look at one another at all.

Chapter 5

Through the Grid

The rain stopped abruptly and the sun came out as they reached the Vale Stables, a sprawling welter of ancient buildings opening off three separate stable yards connected by cobbled alleys. The crumbling brick buildings with the sagging roofs contained, in addition to stalls and loose boxes for more than twenty horses, a blacksmith's shop, an enormous tack-room, a 'hospital' box, a hay barn, and the offices of the Owen-Allerford Riding School.

Behind the stables were the two indoor riding rings used by the Equitators; a vast paddock equipped with permanent show-jumping obstacles and such cross-country obstacles as a ditch-and-rails, two formidable Irish banks, and a water jump; and what looked at first to Dinah's bewildered eyes like a long grape arbour without vines. She stared, uncomprehending, at the high posts and rustic rails that enclosed the narrow alley to a height of seven or eight feet, and only then observed that there were further solid oak rails *across* the lane every few feet, at staggered heights.

'That,' Roger said cheerfully, nodding at the arbour, 'is known as the Grid. Formidable-looking thing, isn't it? One wants to stay in the plate going through there; there's not much chance of coming unstuck from the saddle without knocking against something jolly hard . . . I say, we *are* in luck – here comes old Jock with his W.P.s to bash 'em about!'

Jock Woods was, in fact, not at all old; he was a lean and wiry Scotsman of possibly thirty who had, as a Royal

Marine corporal, once been a member of the British Pentathlon Team. Now, as Stud Groom for the Owen-Allerford School, Jock was also in charge of instructing the Working Pupils as well as schooling the horses kept in the Vale Stables. The Working Pupils were also preparing for the B.H.S. Preliminary Instructor's Certificate, but they paid no tuition and took a full year to prepare for it, and they worked frighteningly hard. Each of them had three horses to groom instead of one, and they had little time off; there was no doubt, however, that the W.P.s, all of whom intended to become genuine professionals, would learn their lessons far more thoroughly than the Horsemasters.

Jock swept off his cap and grinned happily at the Horsemasters, his blue eyes dancing with animation.

'Come to watch my lot get their lumps, have ye, now?' he greeted them cheerfully. 'Well, it'll be your turn over the cavallettis any day now, so you're entitled to see how it's done . . . All right, Julie, m'girl, you've got a nice quiet horse today. You shall be the first to set a good example. Feet out of the stirrups and cross 'em over the front of your saddle – the stirrups, not the feet! – and take Mouse into the Grid. Turn her round, drop your reins, fold your arms and – *go*!'

The other four Working Pupils lined their horses up in an even row; the pretty dark-haired girl on the plump grey mare grimaced and waved weakly at the Horsemasters, who waved back and watched, round-eyed, as she crossed her empty stirrups over the front of her saddle and rode with dangling feet into the end of the arbour. The grey spun round in a complete turn as Julie dropped her reins on the mare's neck and folded her arms across her chest, and then the mare gathered herself and sprang for the first cross-pole, and went racing down the narow alley between the oak rails in a series of bucketing rabbit-jumps while the girl on her back, arms folded and feet dangling, rocked low over her neck at each surging leap.

'I can't *look*!' Jill gasped, and gripped Dinah's arm until her fingers bit into it. 'She'll be *killed*; it's *murder*! No reins and no stirrups, and no way to fall without slamming into those rails . . . !'

But miraculously, before Dinah's horrified eyes the grey mare came out of the other end in a final mighty leap, and the dark-haired Julie was still in the saddle; she gathered up her reins and wheeled the mare about and rode back to the others laughing delightedly, her cheeks rosy. And at once another girl rode forward with her feet dangling out of the stirrups, guiding a tall bay horse into the Grid and wheeling him round on his haunches.

'You mean *we* have to –!' Dinah said faintly, and shut her eyes as the big bay snorted and launched himself forward and went tearing down the alley as hard as he could go. 'Oh, *no*! No, I can't; I *never* –!'

She heard a hollow ringing thud and a muffled clatter, and her eyes flew open; the bay had toppled one of the cross-poles but was bounding on without slackening his pace, and the girl was still on his back, arms folded, crouching low. And then the bay exploded out at the end of the Grid and the girl straightened and reached for her reins; and in that instant the big horse put in one extra jump over nothing at all, and the girl on his back went flying through the air to land rolling and tumbling in the mud.

The bay horse, loose, kicked up his heels and raced, head down and loose reins flapping, all the way round the paddock; he came back to where he had started and stopped, looking around him with a mildly puzzled expression, and lowered his head to crop a mouthful of grass unconcernedly while Jock Woods walked slowly over to him and reached to hold his reins. The girl was on her hands and knees now, shaking her head; she had lost her velvet cap and her long blonde hair hung loose. And then, before anyone could run to her, she was on her feet and picking up her cap, and then trotting over to take the bay from Jock.

'Sorry, Jock!' she said in a quite unshaken voice. 'He always *does* put in one for luck; I should've known ... Could you give me a leg up, please? He's terribly tall ...'

Dinah let her breath out in an explosive sigh and felt Jill's iron grip on her arm relax.

'Ouch!' Peanuts breathed, 'what an absolute purler to take on hard ground! Y'know, I don't think I'm going to like this part of the Course, actually ...'

Roger was watching Jock boost the blonde girl back into her saddle; he turned his head and murmured mildly:

'Better on the ground in the clear than in the Grid, *that's* where you don't want to fall if you can help it ... And that wasn't a bad fall, actually; it looks a lot worse than it feels. Gillian's had plenty of worse falls, hunting; she knows how to fall loose, and that's what counts. When you feel yourself going, just relax all over; there's nothing you can do to save yourself anyway, and if you get all stiffened up struggling against it, you can break something.'

Dinah shuddered; she said weakly:

'*You* may think that wasn't such a bad fall, but I hope I *never* have to take one like it!'

Roger regarded her soberly for a moment. He said, very quietly:

'You will, y'know. Nobody learns to ride without falling, and nobody goes on riding without going on falling. Nobody in the world. No matter how good you get, you'll *still* have a fall now and then. But it's nothing to be afraid of. Look at Gillian.'

The blonde girl was sitting on her horse at the end of

the line, quite unconcernedly brushing the mud from the sleeves of her hacking jacket while a tall slim girl rode a rangy chestnut into the Grid.

But I *am* afraid of it! Dinah thought, shivering. She felt as though her stomach were full of butterflies. She said plaintively, hopefully:

'David never has a fall, and neither does Bee Bye. And how about the Major? Or Captain Pinski? Or Jock?'

'They all *have*,' Roger repeated stubbornly, 'and they all will again. People make mistakes, and so do horses, and you can't expect to put an 8-stone girl on a thousand-pound horse and let 'em go belting over the countryside together without something going wrong once in a while. But people hardly ever get killed in falls from horses, Dinah; usually one doesn't even get hurt. You have to accept that you're going to have a fall every now and then, though. Even if you're the Major, or the Captain, or Jock.'

'S'truth!' Jock said, coming up. He took off his cap and ruefully rubbed his head, adding: 'Ye should hae seen me the mornin' comin' off old Marron! Thir-rty years an' more, that horse must be, an' shaky in his poor old legs; but of a nice fresh mornin', he's nappy as a colt. An' *this* mornin' I couldna stay in th' plate; with all my lot' – he indicated the Working Pupils with a sweeping gesture – 'yellin' and cheerin' like the banshees, the old horse put me off, an' solid! An' I've seen the Major come off, too, an' not so long ago, though he doesna come off easy ... the lad Roger is right, Dinah lassie – ye must hae your falls so long as ye ride the brutes. But 'tis not so bad; 'tis rather fun, y'know – ye'd not enjoy it near so much were it not for the spice o' danger!'

The chestnut went bucketing down through the Grid, throwing his head high and prancing; he got half-way and slid to a stop on his haunches with all four feet braced, and the tall girl fell forward on to his neck, clutching desperately at his mane to keep from falling off. The chestnut spun wildly, banging his rump against the rails so that the whole arbour shook, his eyes rolling wildly, but there was no way out except straight ahead over the rest of the jumps, and not room enough in the narrow alley to turn round.

'Ride him, Primrose!' Jock whooped, and bent double, roaring with laughter. 'Sit on his head, if ye don't like th' feel of th' saddle, but ride him out o' there, girl!'

The tall girl's cap fell off and rolled in the mud beneath the chestnut's feet, but somehow she worked her way back to the saddle. Flushed and dishevelled, her mouth wide open and her eyes alight, she drummed the horse's sides with her heels, yelling fiercely, urging him on. And suddenly the chestnut gave up his rebellion; he gathered himself and jumped off his hocks and took the remaining crosspoles in a series of slow, deliberate, steady jumps.

'Nothin' to it!' Jock howled as the tall girl collected her reins and turned her horse to trot back to the end of the line. 'Who's next? Come on, there, Frenchy girl; *allez-vous-y*!'

He sprinted forward as the next girl rode forth, and fished between the rails with his stick to retrieve Primrose's velvet cap; brushing it off on his sleeve as he came, he strolled back and handed it up to her.

'You *have* had a fall or two, Dinah!' Jill whispered consolingly, 'and you took 'em jolly well, too! No need to look like that; it'll just be more of the same ...'

But the butterflies only fluttered the more wildly in Dinah's stomach; staring in horrified fascination at the unyielding oak rails of the Grid and the hard-packed earth where the blonde Gillian had been hurled, she thought that it would *not* be the same at all. And, striving to reassure herself that perhaps it wouldn't be any worse after all, she recalled her first fall in the Covered School – the first time she had ever fallen off a horse in her life.

That had been from Cotton Socks, of all horses; quiet, steady, smooth-gaited old Cotton Socks, who hated jumping and was sometimes ill-tempered in stable but was absolutely reliable on the ride. And it had all happened so quickly she hadn't had time to be scared or even startled; the Major had commanded, while they were trotting round the school in file, 'Prepare to canter ... now *sit* down; *cease* rising – you *cannot* prepare your horse to canter while you are rising to the trot! *Cease* rising and get *down* in your saddle; and ... *Can-n-n-ter-r-r!*'

And somehow, in trying to remember everything at once, Dinah must have lost her balance; in any case, as Cotton Socks gathered himself and launched into the rocking gait of the canter from the hard jarring one of the trot, she was suddenly no longer on his back, not even right side up. There was only an instant's incredulous sensation of being upside-down and slowly turning over, floating through the air as in a dream; and then the dream ended with a soft thudding jolt and she was rolling on her shoulders in the dark-brown yielding thickness of the sand and sawdust.

She had scrambled to her feet instantly, hastily; she hadn't even lost her hat, though she'd dropped her stick. She had picked that up instinctively, and realized that the Ride had halted and that it was her fault that all thirteen of the others were sitting their horses at a standstill along the walls, and the Major was striding towards her slapping his boot with his stick. Cotton Socks was standing right where he'd been when she fell off, and Dinah took two steps and caught his reins; the Major gave her a leg up without a word. And it wasn't until the Ride was moving again, and she had trotted Cotton Socks half-way round the school, that her heart had stopped racing and the

blood in her veins quit tingling enough for her to realize
that she had actually fallen off a horse! And by that time,
of course, since it hadn't actually hurt at all, there was
nothing to be frightened of . . .

And her second fall had been even easier; it really
hardly counted as a fall at all, although Mercy Hale had
collected Dinah's 10p for the Olympic Fund. That had
been during the first jumping lesson in the Covered
School, when Nutmeg had unexpectedly refused to jump
over a rail just one foot off the ground, and Dinah had lost
her balance again and come off. But she had landed on her
feet, with her reins in her hand, and again she hadn't even
had time to realize she was coming off the horse until she
found herself standing in the sand and sawdust beside him,
feeling thoroughly silly and embarrassed.

But *this*, Dinah thought apprehensively, watching the
last of the Working Pupils spur her horse forward as the
little French girl emerged unscathed from the Grid; *this*
wasn't the same thing at all! It was one thing to fall off a
horse who wasn't doing anything much or going very fast,
and land in six inches of soft sand and sawdust; it would
be something else entirely to be slammed into those oak
rails or catapulted on to that hard ground by a horse
bounding over those cross-rails just as hard as he could go!
And with no reins and stirrups and no control over the
horse at all . . .

Shuddering, Dinah could see herself being loaded on to
a stretcher, while an ambulance stood by and all the
Horsemasters watched in funereal silence . . . And then
suddenly she giggled at the absurdity of herself, thinking,
Boy, am I glad none of these kids can read my feeble
mind!

But the feeling of dread persisted as she watched the rest
of the W.P.'s lesson, and she was very quiet as she strolled
with the rest back towards the stables when it was over.

'Starting this week,' Roger said conversationally as they walked, 'we shall be riding the Vale horses quite a lot, mixed up with our own. Aside from Trocadie and old Kitty, of course; they're for beginners, so we shan't see them any more. But we might as well have a look at the others while we're here, don't you think?'

'True?' Jill demanded. 'Why, Roger? I mean, why ride the Vale horses? What's wrong with our own? Golly, we're just getting to *know* 'em!'

'And that,' Roger said mildly, 'is why. The Major feels we're getting to know 'em, too, so now we've got to ride some we *don't* know. Mr Ffolliott says this is the week. The School policy is that the way to learn to ride *any* horse that may come along is to ride as many different horses as possible. And quite right, too, I should think.'

'It figures,' Bee Bye said thoughtfully. It was the first word Bee Bye had spoken all afternoon, Dinah suddenly realized, ever since she had flared up at David. 'But what happens to our horses while we're riding these? Will the Equitators get 'em? I don't like to think of some Hyde Park rider bumping round on my poor old Booty!'

Roger shrugged to indicate he didn't know, and Peanuts said suddenly, 'Look – Jock's calling us!'

Jock was, indeed; standing outside the blacksmith's shop and waving his cap, he was wildly beckoning them on. They broke into a run together and, when they pulled up breathless, Jock said, grinning with pleasure:

'Got a little treat for you lot, if you'd like to join mine. Ye've been writin' down all th' symptoms of everythin' that can happen to a horse; now happen ye'd like to see the real thing? For the vet's just come, an' I've a horse wi' lampas, an' we're goin' to operate. 'Tis a thing ye should see, to know about!'

The hospital box was in a walled-off end of the hay barn, well away from the stables to permit isolation of any

horse with a contagious disease. Four of the Working
Pupils were ranged along one wall, waiting, while Jock
Woods conferred with the veterinary surgeon in another
corner. The vet was a roly-poly little man with a red face
and white hair; he looked, Dinah thought, like a smiling,
beardless Santa Claus.

The Horsemasters filed in and joined the Working
Pupils along the wall out of the way; as they took their
places, whispering greetings to the others, the dark-haired
Julie who had been first through the Grid on the grey
mare came in, leading a bright bay horse with a fine
head and dark, intelligent eyes.

'Shall I tie him, Jock?' Julie asked, and Jock turned
away from the vet and came towards her, answering:

'No. Ye can hold him, so; 'twill be better.' Addressing
the row of spectators along the wall, he raised his voice a
little and said: 'Now lampas is a swollen condition in the
roof of the mouth; ye'll usually see it in a young horse just
cuttin' his permanent teeth. An' generally ye'll give a laxative diet an' a little Epsom salts in the drinkin' water an'
it'll clear up by itself. But we've done all that with this
little horse an' it *hasn't* cleared up; his mouth hurts him
an' he doesna greet his feed wi' a glad cry of a mornin', so
we must operate. Ye can come forward one at a time now,
an' put your hands to it an' feel what it's like, an' one day
when ye hae a young horse off his feed ye'll know what to
look for. You, Dinah . . .'

Dinah stepped forward and Jock took the bay's nose in
both hands and pulled his mouth open. The bay pulled
back, resisting, and then stood quietly. Rather gingerly,
Dinah put her hand into his mouth and felt the ridged
roof with her fingers; there was a great spongy swelling behind the front teeth, which did not seem to meet properly,
the enlarged upper ones protruding over the lowers.

'This horse has a parrot mouth,' Jock remarked, 'which might be a contributin' cause to his havin' lampas, d'ye think, Doctor? Anyway, wi' teeth like these he's not too good a feeder anyway, the poor little chap; we canna hae him wi' a swollen mouth as well! All right, Dinah; you, Roger, come up here.'

'A tendency to lampas does seem to go with parrot mouth,' the old vet agreed as Dinah went back to her place wiping her hand absently on her skirt and Roger stepped forward to feel the horse's swollen mouth, 'at least I see a good number of parrot-mouthed horses with it. Now, what we'll do here is simply lance the roof of the mouth to reduce the swelling, and then you'll keep him on the laxative diet and I'll give you an additive for his feed to tone up his blood a bit . . .'

When they had all in turn felt the swelling curiously, the vet stepped up and nodded to Jock, who in turn nodded to Julie. Julie took up the slack in the rope attached to the bay's stall collar and braced herself in case he should jump back; Jock also braced himself and forced the bay's mouth wide open. The plump, little white-haired man moved with astonishing agility; his hand seemed to dart at the horse's mouth and instantly withdraw, and he turned away without, apparently, having touched the horse at all.

But a spurt of bright blood suddenly crimsoned Jock's sleeve, and scarlet drops spattered on to the golden straw at his feet; the bay horse stood perfectly still for a moment and then abruptly wrenched free of Jock's restraining hands, snorting a fine crimson spray all over the Stud Groom's shirt front. He threw his head high, rolling his eyes, and Julie braced herself. But the little horse did not rear after all; he dropped his head, with the blood still running from his mouth and dripping on to the clean straw, and stood quite passively, running his long pink tongue out and in again, as though licking his lips to savour the strange new taste.

'That's all there is to that,' the little vet said cheerfully, 'he doesn't care much for the taste, but he should feed well in the morning. Well, I'll be going along. G'bye, all.'

'He never knew he'd been stuck,' Jock muttered, and glanced down ruefully at his ruined shirt, 'but *I* should know it! Ye couldna be a little more tidy aboot it, I dare say?' He turned to grin amiably at the Horsemasters and demanded, 'Will ye know lampas, noo, should ye need to know it one day?'

'I shall never forget it,' plump Jill answered devoutly for all of them, staring round-eyed at the bright scarlet blood spatters on the straw, her face abnormally pale, 'but d'y'know, I think it's quite spoiled my appetite for tea!'

The toothbrush made a fluttering lump in her cheek as Dinah scrubbed vigorously at her teeth; her brown eyes, reflected in the mirror, were worried. Dinner had been a horror, with Bee Bye and David elaborately unaware of each other's presence; the atmosphere in the Blue Room later in the evening, instead of being relaxed and lazy and friendly as it always was, had been thoroughly uncomfortable from the moment David had come in and Bee Bye, without a word, had got up and gone out.

Sighing, Dinah decided reluctantly that she would *have* to talk to Bee Bye, although it certainly wasn't going to be easy, knowing Bee Bye's prickly temper as she did. But this was too hard on all the others, just to let it go and hope that if you pretended it wasn't happening it would get all right without anyone's having to mention it. And Bee Bye was Dinah's friend; had been Dinah's best friend practically all her life. So it looked as though it was up to Dinah, and no getting away from it . . .

H.—4

But oh! Dinah thought morosely as she padded resignedly down the hall back to their room, I wish I knew how to *begin*!

She didn't have to.

Bee Bye was sitting on the edge of Dinah's bed, staring out the window at the faint rippling patterns of the moonlit sea beyond the paddocks; she whirled round as Dinah entered the room and cried:

'Dinah, I can't *help* it; I can't *stand* him! I *know* he's always perfectly polite and nice to everybody, and I *know* everybody else likes him, and I *know* I've acted like a perfect beast, but I *simply* . . . *cannot* . . . *stand* . . . *David* . . . *Perrin*! He just – just rubs me the wrong way, somehow; every time I look at him I want to – to hit him with something! And no matter what he says, the minute he opens his mouth I disagree with him! I've never in my entire life *instinctively* disliked anyone before, but I – I – I – Oh, Dinah, I just plain simply *can't* go and apologize to him. It would just kill me!'

'Well, you ought to,' Dinah said, leaning against the bureau and looking down at Bee Bye's troubled face. 'You've been absolutely lousy to him, you know, and he's never given you one single reason to be.'

'I know it,' Bee Bye murmured miserably, 'but I just *can't*. I just can't help it.'

'It's kind of rough on the others, though,' Dinah said, and took a deep breath and added, 'Look, Bee Bye – we've been friends for a long time, and whether you're right or wrong, where you go, I go. In this case I think you're wrong, but . . . well, for the sake of the other kids, if you and David can't get along, don't you think you and I better ask Mercy to transfer us to Red Ride? Everyone really *cares* about going to these Hunter Trials, and if we're quarrelling among ourselves, our Ride's going to –'

'*No!*' Bee Bye protested harshly, her eyes wide and then

suddenly narrow as she set her jaw and said, 'there's nothing on that List that says you get demerits for not liking somebody. And *I* care about going to the Trials, too, and so does David – and our Ride's going to go! We can lick that other bunch, no hands. And you don't have to worry about me, any of you; I'll work with David or anybody else, and I'll do the best I know how. You don't have to be in l-love with somebody to work with him!'

'I guess you don't,' Dinah agreed, 'although I think it'd help Blue Ride's morale in general if you could kind of pretend you didn't hate the poor guy so ... Tell me, old buddy-buddy, just what *is* it about David that gets your back up so?'

'I just don't *know*!' Bee Bye answered helplessly. 'He's just so – so darned cocksure; every single thing he ever does or says, he does as though naturally there's only one *right* thing to do and naturally this is it ... I don't know, he's just so sure of himself, he just thinks he's so darned good!'

'Well, he *is* good,' Dinah said reasonably, 'and if you mean his riding, for example – why, he's been riding all his life, riding to hounds and riding point-to-point races and he was on the British Army show-jumping team while he was in Germany. Why shouldn't he know he's good, or why should he pretend not to know it? And anyway *you're* just as good as he is, and he's five years older than you are!'

'But I'm *not*!' Bee Bye wailed. 'I'll get my fall any day now, you'll see! And he'll *never* come off, the – the *monster*! And while I'm grovelling in the mud he'll vault gracefully off his horse to help me up, like a perfect little English gentleman – *and I'll swear I'll murder him on the spot in cold blood!*'

Chapter 6

A Great Dressage Expert

Captain Stefan Pinski was a small, spruce, elegant man in his fifties, dapper in beautifully-cut breeches and immaculate boots and a jaunty little hat with a feather in it. He had very bushy eyebrows and piercing grey eyes beneath them; he also had a terrifyingly loud voice and a volatile, not to say hysterical, temperament. When you failed to execute a command properly in the Captain's dressage class, the Captain screamed at you as though your incredible and incomparable stupidity had finally driven him, a patient and forbearing man, beyond the limits of human endurance. It was enough to make you wish a hole would open in the earth beneath you, and drain you and your horse to China in a torrent of sand and sawdust. And it was small consolation to know that none of your colleagues came any closer than you to meeting Captain Pinski's exacting standards.

The Captain, of course, had some justification for finding fault with the horsemanship of the Horsemasters of Owen-Allerford School. The Captain was, in fact, among the great dressage experts of the world; he had won nearly a thousand international trophies as the champion of Poland before the War, when he had been the scion of an old and rich and aristocratic family and the descendant of a long line of superb horsemen. Unfortunately the Captain could no longer afford to train and maintain horses for himself, nor to compete in international events; he had barely got out of Poland alive ahead of the advancing enemy armies and had not managed to bring with him a penny of his fortune, nor even his trophies.

The Captain was a gentleman, however, and gentlemen do not whine. He never complained about his lot as a dressage instructor at Owen-Allerford School, although he very seldom got a chance to instruct a pupil sufficiently advanced to benefit from the full extent of his expert knowledge; in fact, on the whole he rather liked teaching the clumsy but determined and courageous young Horse-masters as much as he could. He liked them all, and he was punctiliously polite and friendly to them whenever he met any of them – *except* during class hours.

During his lessons, however, the Captain's zeal for per-fection seemed to take possession of him; he was a dedi-cated man, and he could not help shrieking in outraged protest when he saw something being done wrong that was so beautiful when done right . . .

'No, *no, NO!*' The Captain was screaming now, his face flushed and contorted. 'It is not like that, the halt, Miss Simms! Regard, *look* the position of the horse! This posi-tion, it *does not exist*, Miss Simms! When I tell you *halt*, you mus' halt where I say, and your horse mus' halt stand-ing square, with all his four feet under him! I have tol' you, at the E marker, *halt*. And look, Miss Simms, where you are! *Where you are!*'

Bee Bye sat motionless and erect atop an enormous and ridiculously ugly fat cob called Freddie Fox, one of the horses they had hacked up from the Vale Stables for this morning's ride. And big, fat Freddie stood motionless against the Covered School wall just under the E marker in the centre of the long side of the school, twitching his absurd tuft of bobbed tail and working a long rubbery lower lip like a man talking to himself. Dinah, next in the waiting line of frozen, expressionless Horsemasters, squirmed with embarrassment for poor Bee Bye as her friend sat silent and helpless beneath the torrent of the Captain's scorn.

'You are wahn foot an' more beyond the E marker!' the little man screamed. 'When you stop, your *knee* mus' be exactly opposite the marker; it is to lose points in competition if you pass the marker! An' your horse, how he stands! He is not square, weeth wahn foot at each corner; *no!* He is off-balance. It is not correct! An' you, Miss Simms, when you stop he drops his head, your horse, an' you hold so stiff the reins you fall forward on his neck! You *must ... not ... be ... ever ... stiff!*'

He paused, and seemed to labour to draw breath; then he said quite calmly, almost quietly:

'All right, Miss Simms It was not bad. You will join please the Ride, an' we will try the next rider.'

Bee Bye rammed her heels into the fat cob's sides, and he stepped off in a shambling, shuffling trot, still twitching his docked stub of tail; her face expressionless, she rode round the school and guided Freddie into place at the end of the waiting line.

'Dressage,' Captain Pinski addressed the class, still in his calm quiet voice, 'it is the art of *invisible, perfect* control of the horse by the rider. The hands, the legs – they mus' work always *independently*, always gently, always invisibly. An' they mus' make the horse do always *exactly* what he is asked to do. To poosh, to haul, to lose the balance – in the hunting field it is all right, perhaps, but in dressage competition, *no!* An' to school well a good horse, *or* a good rider, dressage is necessary ... Very well, we shall have Miss Wilcox, on Mouse! Miss Wilcox, will you ride one time roun' the school, please, at the ordinary trot? And will you stop, please, at the E marker? An' will you then execute a turn in the forehand, and *immediately* walk on? Miss – Wilcox!'

Dinah had hacked the grey mare up from the Vale, a

mile and a half at a walk and an easy trot over the paved road; aside from that she had never ridden Mouse before. Indeed, she had only seen the mare once before, when the Working Pupil named Julie had ridden her – safely, Dinah recalled thankfully – through the Grid. Now she breathed a hurried prayer and spurred the grey into a comfortable trot, frantically checking on everything she could remember as the mare obediently trotted round the school: Hands low and steady; right! Just enough tension on reins to keep arch in horse's neck; *right*! Heels down – oops! *Right*, now! Rising to the correct shoulder; *right*! Body erect but not stiff, lower body and legs independent of upper; *right*! Eyes straight ahead, look between the horse's ears . . .

The E marker was three strides ahead, and Dinah dropped her seat into the saddle and sat tight, ceasing to rise to the mare's trot. She closed her fists firmly on the already taut reins and felt the mare's head come back to her as Mouse broke her trot to a walk; at the same time Dinah applied her legs firmly and felt Mouse bring her quarters up under her as she halted, neck still deeply flexed, chin tucked in. Dinah eased the tension on the reins a little bit, and the mare stretched her neck comfortably but did not move. The E marker was, she saw, still a little way ahead of her knee, but –

'It . . . was . . . *correct*!' the Captain screamed, and Dinah was suffused with a warm glow; there were actually tears in her eyes. Captain Pinski was seldom pleased with anyone; when he did give out a word of praise you felt as though you had been decorated . . . And now for the turn on the forehand!

Holding her hands low and perfectly still as they were, keeping contact with the mare's mouth but not pulling it either way, Dinah very cautiously slid her right leg back along the wall, close to the grey's side. And well behind the girth she applied her heel once, twice ... and nothing happened. She applied the heel again, a little harder – and Mouse flinched away from it, taking two quick steps sideways into the centre of the school.

'No, *no, NO*!' the Captain was screaming instantly, and now it was Dinah's turn to bow her head to the storm, shrinking under the sympathetic gaze of all her classmates. 'Eet ees *not* correct, Miss Wilcox; it is – it is *abominable*! With the hands one holds the forehand steady, that is correct; with the legs one moves, so delicately, the quarters in a pivot round the motionless forehand ... but to *kick* the poor horse so that she jumps sideways – no, *no, NO*! It does not exist, this! Go, and join the Ride! Next! Mr Perrin!'

Feeling numb all over, Dinah rode in lonely grandeur round the vast school to take her place in line. But there was a kernel of warmth deep inside her, and it spread, driving the numb disappointment before it. She *had* done half of it right, and anything the Captain said was correct was *correct*. And she would do the turn in the forehand correctly, too, next time ... She gave Mouse a loose rein, and bent forward to pat the mare's neck, murmuring, 'Good girl!'

'Mr Perrin,' Captain Pinski said quietly, 'you will go ordinary trot, please, to the C marker; then you will go sitting trot half-arena; and on returning to the C marker you will canter half-arena; between the C marker and the H marker you will trot, walk, and stop; and you will execute a turn on the haunches. Will you repeat, please, Mr Perrin?'

'Yes, sir!' David called out smartly. 'I am to trot to the C marker, ordinary trot that is; then sitting trot half-arena; then canter in the same circle, half-arena; then trot, walk, and stop before the H marker, and execute a turn on the haunches.'

'It is correct,' the Captain said, nodding. 'You will go now, please, Mr Perrin.'

Dinah was aware of the hush that hung over the school as David coaxed Copper sidling and shying out of the line; Copper did not like leaving the other horses to go off by himself. He picked his front feet up very high, prancing gracefully, and little spurts of dust arose with each prancing step to shimmer in the amber sunlight slanting down from the high windows. It was hot in the Covered School, and the odour of horses was strong; a little trickle of perspiration ran down between Dinah's shoulder blades and she wriggled, wishing she could scratch the tickly feeling. She felt drowsy now; she wished the lesson was over . . .

David was trotting down the long side of the school now, rising with negligent grace and assurance to the quick rhythm of Copper's smart trot. He looked, Dinah thought, as though he had been born in the saddle; he rode like part of the horse. Copper went straight up into the corner and bent himself double turning into the short side of the school; that was David again, controlling the difficult horse properly instead of letting Copper cut off a corner as he would have done with almost any of the rest of them. And now at the C marker, in the middle of the short side of the school, David stopped rising and sat quite comfortably deep in his saddle without bouncing at all, while Copper shortened his stride a little but did not slacken his trotting pace.

They went round in a smooth sweeping circle that took up precisely one-half of the school, the tall copper-coloured horse and the slender red-headed boy looking as though they were fused together. And precisely as Copper passed the C marker again, in response to David's invisible command, Copper struck off into a rocking, perfectly collected canter. They went round again, cantering, and as they returned to the C marker Copper broke his canter to trot a couple of steps and then to a walk, and then stopped four-square opposite the H marker.

'Oh, *perfect*!' someone breathed at Dinah's right, and the silence fell again. Copper stood motionless; David, in the saddle, sat still as a statue. They waited, and nothing happened; then Copper tossed his head suddenly, and shifted his front feet restlessly. And instantly the Captain was screaming:

'No, *no*, No! It is *not* correct, Mr Perrin; *eet . . . ees . . . not . . . correct*! You mus' use *loose* leg, *living* leg; not dead, stiff leg like block of wood! You mus' feel *with* horse, an' horse will feel with you; you cannot *keeck* horse with clumsy stiff leg like not part of you at all! You are stiff, Mr Perrin, stiff, *stiff*, *STIFF*! You mus' be flexible! I have told you so many times before; is it possible that you learn *nothing* here, Mr Perrin? Why you do thees theeng? Do you learn *nothing*?'

And suddenly David's immobile face went white as a sheet; without warning it crumbled, and his unshakable self-control crumbled with it. With a single violent ungraceful motion David vaulted out of the saddle and landed spraddle-legged in the sawdust still clutching Copper's reins, and facing the captain, who had fallen silent in shock. Recovering his balance, David drew himself erect; he stood at attention and stared straight ahead woodenly as a sentry and replied in a voice that shook a little with emotion:

'Apparently not, sir. I have learned nothing, sir. I request your permission to withdraw from the class, sir!'

Someone in the line of Horsemasters gasped, and someone else instantly hissed, 'Sh-h-h!' For a long frozen moment the tableau at the other end of the school remained motionless and silent, David standing rigidly at attention, holding the reins of his statuesque horse and staring unwinking at Captain Pinski, who stood equally rigid and stared back as though he could not quite believe what he had heard.

And then the Captain moved. His right hand came half-way up and stopped, as though he had started to salute and suddenly remembered he was not in uniform; he made, instead, a funny jerky little bow in David's direction. And he said, in a very quiet voice that nevertheless carried to the Horsemasters at the other end of the school :

'Permission granted, Mr Perrin – *if* you still request it after I have tol' you, please, a story . . .

'Many years ago, Mr Perrin, when I am young man like you, I am lieutenant in Polish Cavalry. I am, because it is thing to do in Poland; it is profession – *only* profession – for young men of good family to follow. And also, all of my friends are likewise lieutenants in Polish Cavalry, all the young men I have known all my life; always we have ridden together an' hunted together, an' in peacetime cavalry we will do only more of the same. It is understood. An' *always*, all of my life, I have had many many horses of my father's stables; *always* I have been best rider of us all.

'So, we have dressage instruction one day, all of us lieu-tenants together, all the sons of all the best families of Poland, you understand? It is like this lesson, in Covered School. An' when it is my turn to ride, I ride as best I can; an' when I am finish' our Instructor screams at me – *in front of all my friends*! – he screams, "Lieutenant Pinski, you have hands like blacksmith!" '

The little man paused, and his face screwed up into an agonized expression, remembering that long-ago bitter-ness; he took a deep breath and sighed, and went on quietly :

'What do I do? I do what you do, Mr Perrin. I dismount my horse; I salute; I click my heels, so!'

He snapped to attention, the heels of his immaculate

boots clicked sharply together; he threw a smart military salute, and continued:

'*And* I say, "Sir, Lieutenant Pinski requests the Colonel's permission to withdraw from this class, preparatory to resigning his commission, sir!" And my Colonel tells me, "Lieutenant Pinski, you do *not*, perhaps, have hands like blacksmith, but you are very insolent young man and also you are a great fool. And if you do not mount your horse immediately, you will not be in two more years champion of Poland!" So . . .'

The little Captain shrugged, and finished almost inaudibly:

'So I mount again my horse – and in two years I am champion of Poland! And now, Mr Perrin, if you permit that I ride your horse one little minute before you withdraw . . . ?'

David stood aside, moving as though in a trance; the Captain mounted Copper gracefully and sat quite still. He moved not a muscle that anyone could see, but all at once the big sorrel seemed, without budging from his place, to come vibrantly alive as he had never looked alive before. His ears pointed alertly forward, his neck arched, and he tucked his chin in, mouthing his bit; he seemed to flex every muscle in his body, quivering with eagerness.

'We will walk,' the Captain said, and Copper stepped off, walking as though each separate footstep were a thing to be executed with absolute precision. Something like an icy finger touched the back of Dinah's neck and sent a chill all through her; she felt that she had never before perceived the potential beauty of a horse in motion.

'We will trot,' the Captain said, and again in trotting Copper seemed to extend each leg separately and hesitate a fraction of a second at the completion of that perfect motion before commencing the next. And the little man perched high on his back sat perfectly still and expressionless, but just as the horse's body seemed to come alive for the first time, so the man's body seemed to flow into that of the horse and become a part of it.

'We will canter, and then extended canter, and then collected canter,' the Captain said, and from a graceful rocking canter Copper was suddenly tearing round the confined space of the school at a terrifying pace, surely out of control; and as suddenly rocking calmly round in his short collected canter again.

'He has not bad gaits, this horse,' the Captain said mildly, bringing Copper down to a short trot and sitting it without effort. 'He is not trained dressage horse, of course, but I think we will *try* half-pass from sitting trot . . .'

And then Copper seemed to be doing a dainty tricky dance step diagonally across the school, his body perfectly parallel to the long wall but travelling on a long diagonal line towards the opposite corner as he actually *crossed* one leg in front of the other with each jaunty, dancing sideways step.

'And now,' the Captain said, 'we will do Mr Perrin's turn on the haunches without stopping, from the walk; it is then called pirouette. You will watch, please; you will see that he will turn round and go at once in other direction, but his hind feet will not move out from wall, only his forehand will go round . . .'

Copper did just that, and halted; the Captain sat still for a moment, and then bent forward to slap the big sorrel's neck in praise. He dismounted, and held out Copper's reins to David, who walked dreamily forward and took them.

'Like *that* you will one day ride, Mr Perrin, if you will continue,' the Captain said quietly. 'You will be one day very good rider. You, and Miss Simms; perhaps some of the others as well, but you two certainly. Only you must realize that that day is not yet, and not soon; it is very far off. And one other thing: you do not like when I shout so loud at you, so rude. Very well, I should not like it either. I can understand this. But I *must* shout at you, and I *will* shout at you, and you must forgive. And perhaps you will forgive if you understand this: when I shout, I am excited. And when I am excited, it is because I *know* you can do better than you *are* doing, an' I am impatient that you *be* so good as I know you *can* be! . . . I think now we end this lesson for this day; it is few minutes early still, but we have done enough . . .'

He made his jerky little bow to David again, and at once turned to face the class. Sweeping off his jaunty little hat, he bowed low as he did at the conclusion of every lesson, and as always he called out clearly:

'Thank . . . you very much!'

And with that the Captain about-faced smartly and marched out of the school, leaving behind him a stunned and profoundly thoughtful group of Horsemasters, any one of whom would have died for the little man without a second's hesitation.

In the bright hot sunlight the blue sea was creamed with foaming white; the wooded hills rising steeply beyond the neat meadows on the other side of the road were leafy green. The sunlight cast dappled patterns upon the road itself through the trees that lined it; a little breeze rustled the leaves overhead. Far away a crow cawed raucously and another answered him, jeering, the sound almost drowned out by the clopping of the horses' hooves on hard pavement and the rhythmic creaking of their saddles.

The four Vale horses jogged lazily along abreast, spanning the narrow road; fat, stupid-looking Freddie next to the ditch at the left with Bee Bye riding high and erect in the saddle, and then Dinah on grey Mouse, and Betsy Murphy on the black Nightshade and Toni Harper riding

the rangy dun, Highboy. They rode in silence, each pre-
occupied with her own thoughts; no one had said a word
since they had ridden out of the Covered School to hack
the Vale horses back to their stables, leaving the rest of the
Horsemasters to lead the home horses out. They *would*, of
course, talk about Captain Pinski and this morning's
lesson; they were fairly bursting with it now. But no one
seemed to want to speak just *yet*; it was as though they had
a beautifully wrapped package among them and were not
quite ready to open it.

Dinah glanced sideways at Betsy's faraway, dreaming
face; beyond Betsy, Toni Harper's lips were curved in a
soft smile, her eyes half closed. Fat Freddie had got a little
ahead of Mouse, and Dinah could not see Bee Bye's face;
she urged Mouse on a little, and saw that Bee Bye's eyes
were wide and sparkling, and that her expression was one
of a strange sheepish delight.

Dinah herself felt wonderful; she had a warm glowing
feeling all over inside, and there was no place in the world
she would rather be than clopping lazily along this English
road on a horse, riding with skill and confidence and lov-
ing every minute of it ... and having that wonderful
morning to think about, among her friends. An old lady in
long black skirts was coming towards them riding a bicycle; as they approached, the old lady stopped and dismounted, just in case one of the horses might be frightened
by a moving bicycle, and waved at them as they jogged by.
They all waved gaily back, and that somehow seemed to
break the spell; Betsy Murphy coughed apologetically, and
spoke.

'Poor old David!' she said quite cheerfully, 'I'll bet he
didn't half feel a fool! But *isn't* our little Captain an
absolute wizard?'

'*David*,' Bee Bye said instantly, astonishingly, and the
sheepish expression was suddenly gone entirely, 'is *entirely*

all right! Don't you think it's nice that he's human after all? . . . Oh, do let's trot on, shall we?'

And without waiting for an answer she spurred fat Freddie into a heavy trot, leaving the others to exchange bewildered glances and then string out behind her in single file, trotting briskly along the edge of the ditch through the sunlight-dappled shadows on the road.

Chapter 7

A Terrible Purler

On Sunday morning Dinah was up at six o'clock, and in the stable yard, numb with sleep, by six-fifteen. Blue Ride had double work to do today, two horses apiece to groom; this was Red Ride's weekend off. Enzo Lalli, resplendent in a gaudy tight-fitting striped suit and sharply pointed shoes, had hired a car and departed for London immediately after Saturday lunch; Ingrid and Gretel and Lady Audrey Hughes had gone with him, sharing expenses, while Toni and Betsy and Sally had elected simply to spend a lazy weekend at School, lying late abed.

Racing against time, Dinah watered Corny P. and then Nightingale, estimating with pleasure as she carried in the little dark-grey Arab's water bucket that she should be able to muck out his relatively tidy stall in two trips to the muck heap as opposed to the four she always had to make for Corny P. Swiftly and efficiently she cleared the front of Corny's stall and laid fresh bedding there for him to stand on while feeding; then she flew to Stable One to do the same for Nightingale. The stable work was much easier now; she seemed to be able to get everything done almost automatically, without thinking, and with far less effort.

Even so, she was surprised and pleased to discover that she had both horses ready to be fed, and Mercy had not yet banged on the feed box, shrilling 'Fee-e-eed!' Without hesitation she continued mucking out Nightingale's stall; perhaps she could make one trip to the muck heap before Mercy arrived, and that would be this half of the job half done . . . She gathered up the heavy mucksack and got it on to her back with an effort and staggered off to dump it, listening all the way for the metallic banging and the shrill summons; hurrying back, she glanced at the stable-yard clock and saw that it was, incredibly, ten minutes past seven – ten whole minutes past feeding time, and Mercy Hale hadn't shown up yet! The horses were all restive now. She could hear them all stamping and snorting; Corny P. was positively frantic, sidling all over his stall, rolling his eyes and bitterly protesting his hunger.

'Do you *suppose*,' Peanuts asked in awed delight, 'that Mercy could have overslept? Shouldn't somebody go to see? *I'll* go!'

'You'll not, y'know,' David contradicted her firmly, coming out of Stable Two, 'there's no need. She hasn't overslept; she's out hacking. Pennant's out. So she'll be in any minute, and we'd better get on with it; if Mercy's going to be late for the first time in her life, she'll likely be looking for somebody to take it out on. And don't *anyone* ask innocently if her watch stopped, or we shall have one thousand demerits before the day's out!'

'Yipe!' Peanuts squeaked faintly, and dived back into Pipe Clay's box.

Dinah finished cleaning out Nightingale's stall and made her second trip to the muck heap, while all the horses took to kicking thunderously in their stalls and boxes and whinnying in shrill protest. It was after seven-twenty now. She would go and carry down a bale of clean straw and finish bedding down Nightingale first, she decided, and then start on the big job of mucking out Corny P. But before she could get started for the hay barn, she heard the clatter of a horse's hooves jogging over the brick-paved stable yard; *Mercy!* she thought. And then in the same instant heard the confused shouting break out all over the stables, and dashed out into the stable yard. There was a note of shrill alarm in the voices shouting from Stable Two, and everybody seemed to be running in that direction; Dinah sprinted across the yard to catch up with the others, crowding into the midst of the jostling mob.

There was a horse in the paved aisle between the loose boxes, she saw first; it was crowding up against the iron-barred door to the end box, as though trying to get in. That was Pennant's box. Why, the horse was Pennant, of course! But where was Mercy? Pennant was still saddled, but –

'Must've pulled the bridle off when she fell,' David was saying. 'Look – Pennant's fallen, and hard; somersaulted right end-over-end, from the look of it! Mud here, and she's cut a little here – not bad, that won't hurt anything – *Rog!* Here, you're the best of the lot of us as a vet, you go over Pennant and see what injuries you can find. *Jill!* You run up to the house and get the Major on the phone and tell him Pennant's come in without a bridle and he'd better send someone out to look for Mercy; and then call either Jock Woods or Mr Ffolliott, I don't care which, and get him out here to look the horse over – Now, *jump!*'

Plump Jill jumped, and dashed out at a hard run; Roger had already opened the door and led Pennant into her box; he was pulling her saddle off as David turned to the others and snapped:

'All right, let's get these horses fed! We'll have to help ourselves to corn today; Mercy's got a list of how much each horse gets tacked over the feed box. I'll take care of my two and Roger's, that's Bay Rum and Copper and Cotton Socks and Blue Trout. Dinah, will you feed for Jill as well as your two horses? She has Shadow and Claddagh

Boy. And Peanuts, just get Pennant's feed ready, will you please, but don't give it to her until Jock gets here. All right, let's get *cracking*!'

Bee Bye took a half-step forward impulsively, her face distressed, and reached to touch David's sleeve as she said, 'Can't I hel –?' But David wasn't looking, and he didn't hear her; he was already hustling towards the feed box with swift purposeful strides, and after a moment Bee Bye followed, running as hard as she could. And then for a blurred half-hour Dinah lost track entirely of the sequence of events while she fed four horses and carried straw bales and filled hay nets for two, and then dived out to hear Jill returning and breathlessly reporting that Jock Woods was on his way and the vet would look in on Pennant later, and the Major and Captain Pinski had ridden off each leading a spare horse to look for Mercy. And then Roger put his head in while she was loading Corny P.'s last muck-sack to report that he didn't *think* Pennant was hurt at all, but she must have taken a terrible purler. And as Dinah began vigorously dandy-brushing Corny P., the dark thought nobody had spoken hung over her like a dread weight:

What had happened to Mercy when the horse had fallen with her?

She had just finished grooming Corny P. and was hurrying across the yard to groom Nightingale when Jock Woods arrived; instinctively she swerved to follow Jock into Stable One, to be there when the Stud Groom examined Pennant. But David was there suddenly, barring the way; David was saying in a harsh angry voice:

'All right, everybody, Jock doesn't need any help from us! And we wouldn't be neglecting our work if Mercy were here, so let's get on with it, shall we?'

Abashed, Dinah retreated; as she hurried into Stable One, she heard Jill Taylor say:

'He's right, y'know! Red Ride's off for the weekend; it's us that gets all the demerits that're going!'

And Peanuts Pride murmured, with a catch in her voice:

'Demerits! I almost wish she'd show up and *give* us a few demerits, just so she's all right!'

But when she heard the multiple hoof-beats of approaching horses, some twenty minutes later, Dinah dropped her hoof pick and abandoned Nightingale, racing out into the stable yard as all the others appeared from the various stables. The Major and Mercy were just dismounting outside the yard; Captain Pinski was bringing up the rear, leading a saddled and bridled spare horse.

The Horsemasters of Blue Ride stood back in a silent watchful group as the Major and Mercy hurried into Stable Two; they exchanged a round-eyed glance, and waited silently. Mercy was limping a little and she had a great purple swelling on her chalk-white forehead; she was hatless and her trim hacking jacket was mud-smeared and torn. But she was indisputably alive. The voices of Jock and the Major came indistinctly from the cavernous interior of Stable Two; with one accord Blue Ride moved forward and crowded in, in a concerted rush.

'Now, th' little mare's all right, Mercy!' Jock was saying soothingly. 'The vet is on his way, but I canna find a thing amiss wi' her. She isna lame, nor has she cut herself; she wants a good groomin', an' that'll be the lot!'

'I'll groom her myself!' Mercy said instantly, 'I'll – where's her grooming kit? I want to take care of her myself!'

'Now, there, Mercy,' Jock said, and put a restraining hand on Mercy's arm. 'Ye canna groom a horse the while she's feedin'; ye know better than that! An' look, the appetite she has! Now, you go an' hae yourself a bath, an' –'

'*Feed*!' Mercy exclaimed, and pulled away from Jock's restraining hand. 'I have to – I haven't fed the horses, they haven't been mucked out nor groomed; the yards haven't been done! I have to –'

'It's all done, Mercy,' David said quietly; 'the mucking out and bedding down, that is; we've not quite finished grooming. And we've fed, We decided we'd better feed as soon as Pennant came in and we knew you'd had a fall. Why don't you do as Jock says and go have a bath while we get on the yards? You can inspect when you come back.'

Mercy's blue eyes were dazed and incredulous; she stared at David and then at each of the others in turn. And finally she wet pale lips with the tip of her tongue and said faintly, 'Thank you, David. Thank you, *all* of you. But –'

'All right, Mercy!' the Major commanded briskly, 'that's enough for now; everything seems to be under control here. Go have your bath. *Now.*'

The Major's clipped voice brooked no obstruction and no delay; it galvanized the stunned Mercy into action. Obediently she trotted off, and the Major turned to the Horsemasters, who were beginning to drift back to their work.

'You would probably like to know what happened and how,' the Major said pleasantly. 'Mercy put Pennant at a fallen log, quite a good-sized one, and the mare slipped on take-off and failed to clear it. It was a good solid obstacle; and the mare came down on her head and somersaulted. Mercy kept hold of her reins, but she pulled the bridle off and the mare came home without her. No one's fault, and no one seems to be hurt … And now I've no doubt you'd all like to go back to your work, so I shan't keep you from it. Ah … you did exactly the right thing, all of you. Well done!'

He nodded in dismissal and the Horsemasters got out of

there fast, but as the Major turned away Dinah saw that he was smiling broadly, and his frosty blue eyes were sparkling with pleasure. And she thought, wonderingly, Now, what's *he* got to be so pleased about?

She continued to wonder about that as she went on with grooming Nightingale, brushing out his silky dark-grey coat while he turned his head and nuzzled at her with a velvety nose. He was so delicately made, she thought; he had legs like a deer's, his cannons weren't much thicker than her wrist. Of course Mr Ffolliott said always buy a horse with plenty of bone, meaning thick sturdy leg bones, but Nightingale was so *graceful*. And he wasn't as fragile as he looked, either.

She thought she had finished picking out his feet before Mercy's arrival, but better make sure . . . she picked up a hind foot, the hoof the size of a teacup, and ruefully compared it with Corny P.'s great flat soup plates. Ah, to be able to trade Corny P. for this neat, dainty little horse and have only half as much work to do in the stables! But no good wishing; she was stuck with clumsy, dirty, untidy old Corny . . .

'Yards, everybody! Yards, please!' David was yelling, banging on the feed box just as Mercy did; his light baritone was a startling change from Mercy's shrill piping voice, though. For a moment it sounded as though David was joking, but he wasn't; the work was there to be done. Sighing, Dinah put away Nightingale's grooming kit and went out into the stable yard, dragging her broom behind her.

The hay barn was open on three sides to the summer air, and a few fat flies buzzed sleepily in from the hot sunlight to circle aimlessly in the fragrant shade and zoom out again; a pair of swallows dipped in and vanished in the lofty darkness beneath the stilted roof. Roger and David sat cross-legged in the scattered loose hay in the middle of the floor, face-to-face and a few feet apart; each held one end of an inch-thick rope of twisted hay and was absorbedly twisting handful after handful of hay to add to its length. The other five members of Blue Ride sprawled in the loose hay watching; seated primly erect on the stacked hay bales, looking incongruous in skirts and sweaters and stockings, were Toni Harper and Betsy Murphy and Sally Burnham.

'She looked like death warmed up!' Sally declared. 'We didn't know anything about it, of course; golly, Betsy and Toni were still asleep, and I only woke up when she came stumbling in. Didn't even know it wasn't her room. White as a sheet, and her jacket all torn and muddy, and that horrible lump on her forehead. And she just stood there in a kind of daze, muttering over and over again, "I'll die, I'll really and truly *die* if Pennant's hurt! I *want* to die, I *will* die if I've hurt her!" So I jumped out of bed; I was still half-asleep but waking up fast; I forgot all about it being Sunday and our lie-in. So of course I could see she'd had a fall, and I said, "Mercy, are you all right? Are you hurt?" And she just kept on saying, "I'll *die* if she's not all right!" I tell you, it gave me the creeps!'

'She loves that horse,' Peanuts said in a wondering tone. 'She really and truly *loves* that horse! It's hard to believe Mercy could really love anything, she's so full of meanness, but she really loves Pennant!'

'You wouldn't doubt it,' Betsy agreed, shaking her head, 'if you'd been there when she came in. Sally and Toni and I got her undressed and gave her a bath, and she didn't seem to know what was going on at all; but when we tried to put her to bed she wasn't having any. Not a bit of it! She ran the lot of us out of there, hard as nails and just as nasty as ever, and got herself into her jeans and lit out for the stables as hard as she could go. And that's the last *we* saw of Miss Mercy Hale this morning!'

Roger nodded to David and backed away crab-wise until the rope of twisted hay was stretched taut between them; it was about eight feet long. David squinted at it judiciously and nodded his approval; they had got it to a fairly even thickness throughout its entire length, but it looked spiky and frayed with loose ravels of hay sticking up every few inches.

'Dinah,' David said absently, 'there's a pair of scissors sticking out of my hip pocket. Will you get 'em out, please, and snip off all the loose bits and pieces while we hold this thing together? We can take up your story from there, Betsy. Mercy came belting down to the stables and shut herself in Pennant's box with a grooming kit and tweezers and the iodine bottle, and she stayed in there crooning to Pennant and hunting for imaginary thorns to pick out of her fair skin and grooming her and singing her lullabies until lunch time. She never even bothered to inspect the stables, or the yards, or the horses. She –'

'Lucky thing for Blue Ride!' Sally snorted derisively. 'Wouldn't you *know* the day we're off and these clumsy ignoramuses – or would the plural of ignoramus be igno-rami! It *does* sound Latin – are doing their usual slipshod job of leaving the stables filthy and the horses half groomed, Mercy would fall on her head and spare 'em a couple hundred demerits?'

'If you can find *one* thing in those stables to demerit, Sally Burnham,' Jill cried, rising to the bait. 'I'll – I'll –'

Dinah had fished the scissors out of David's pocket; she hesitated, puzzled, and looked from one boy to the other, but their faces seemed relaxed and entirely serious. Obediently, she snipped off a few protruding bits of hay, and the boys turned their rope over so that she could trim its underside; she glanced suspiciously at them again, but they seemed to be quite matter-of-fact about the silly job, whatever it was. So, shrugging, Dinah snipped busily away until the entire eight-foot length of the hay rope was neat and clean and no longer bristly. The others had all fallen silent now, and were watching curiously as Dinah sat back on her knees with her feet tucked under her.

'Thanks, Dinah,' David murmured absently and crawled a foot or two towards Roger. Carefully, he gathered in his end of the rope and made two side-by-side loops in it; holding the looped end tightly with both hands, he murmured, 'Okay, Rog.'

Roger thereupon advanced upon David, still holding his end of the rope; he began to wind it tightly in and out, round and between David's two loops until he had woven them tightly together so that they almost disappeared, and then he tucked the remaining short end through one loop and into the other, and stood back.

'*Et voilà!*' David cried. 'That's French, Adrienne? Now we wet this well and bang it against the wall a few times, and we shall have the handsomest hay wisp any horse ever got strapped with! And not a bit too good for my Bay Rum, at that; ours is a disgrace! Anyone else for a new wisp, while we experts are in the manufacturing business?'

He held up the neatly woven, symmetrical block of hay triumphantly, and Bee Bye said at once:

'Me! But let's try that, Dinah; I bet we can make one as good as that. I saw everything they did!'

Dinah promptly sat down in the hay facing Bee Bye; as they began to twist a handful of hay together, Peanuts cried:

'Come on, then, Jill; let's have a go! It looks rather a neat trick, that!'

David and Roger exchanged a solemn wink and silently removed themselves from the scene; for a time there was

silence as the four girls frowned in concentration over the
steadily growing lengths of their two ropes of hay.

'There!' Bee Bye said at last, critically. 'That looks
about the right length, doesn't it? . . . What'd you do with
his scissors, Dinah?'

'In my shirt pocket,' Dinah said. 'Adrienne! Come shear
this beast, will you?'

But somehow it didn't work. Adrienne sheared the rope
and Dinah made two loops and Bee Bye wove them together, and the whole thing fell apart; doggedly they
started all over twisting a new rope while the same thing
happened to Peanuts and Jill. And again Adrienne
sheared, giggling, and this time Bee Bye made the loops
and Dinah carefully wove the block, and succeeded in
making a horrible-looking lumpy thing twice too big to be
held in one hand.

'Well, it stays *together*,' she murmured dubiously, 'but
somehow I feel there's more to this trick than meets the
eye . . . Here, you can have it, Bee Bye.'

'Thanks,' Bee Bye said shortly, 'if I hit poor old Booty
just once with that thing it'd drive him to his knees . . . I
sure do hate to admit to those darned boys that we can't do
it, though; did you see the sneers on their odious faces
when we started? How are you two doing?'

'Hopelessly,' Peanuts said dolefully, and then bright-
ened, 'but I *have* got an idea! We don't bed down until
four, and it's not two-thirty; we've plenty of time to walk
to the Vale and get Jock or Mr Ffolliott or one of the W.P.s
to show us how to make a super wisp. And who's to know
when we start bashing our nags about with 'em tomorrow,
that we had to go for help?'

'A hay barn in the Vale,' Adrienne murmured drowsily,
'is much the same to me as a hay barn here, except that it
is one mile and a half away. So I think I will stay where I
am and sleep in the hay a little; it smells nice. You will

wake me when it is time to bed down and do the yards again, no?'

Yawning, she toppled over into the fragrant hay, and stretched luxuriously and sighed, and slept. It made Dinah feel sleepy just to look at Adrienne; for a moment she could not decide whether to lie here dozing in the hay or go with the others, already tramping purposefully out of the barn. But she was not quite sleepy enough to risk missing anything, she decided, and got hastily to her feet to follow.

Sundays! she thought in mild exasperation. The only day in the week we don't ride, and you'd think we'd be glad of the rest. But even doing double stable duty, the day seems a week long; I wish it was tomorrow!

Chapter 8

'Off You Go!'

On Monday morning Mercy was entirely herself again, as chilly and unfriendly and unpleasant as ever. She drove the Horsemasters shrilly through their stable chores, waspishly finding fault with everything they did. She tongue-lashed David rudely for visiting Copper's box to chat with Roger while Roger was grooming the big sorrel, although David had already finished grooming and strapping Bay Rum; she gave Ingrid demerits for using too much bedding, and Adrienne an equal number for using not enough; she managed to find something critical and sarcastic to say to every one of them until they lost whatever ebullience they might have had at the beginning of the morning, and lapsed into a sullen and resentful silence, redoubling their efforts to anticipate and eliminate the cause for Mercy's next complaint.

Dinah could *not* get Corny P.'s near hind foot clean; it seemed to have some ragged, horribly smelly black substance adhering to the frog. The odour almost made her gag, and she could not get it off; at length she managed to get the sole scraped clean and white enough to be sure that the rotten-smelling raggedness was actually part of the frog of Corny's hoof, flapping loose like thick peeling skin. It looked sickening and smelled worse than that, and something obviously had to be done about it. Reluctantly, Dinah went and found Mercy, and Mercy stared at her bleakly and said curtly:

'Sounds like thrush, doesn't it? You *have* had thrush in Mr Ffolliott's lectures, haven't you? Let's take a look –'

She trotted briskly across the stable yard with Dinah hurrying to keep up; Peanuts Pride, passing, stared curiously and followed at a discreet interval. And Betsy Murphy, observing from the water trough, set down her bucket and joined the procession. When anyone actually *sought out* Mercy Hale, especially on a morning like this one, something was up; by the time Mercy had put down Corny's foot and looked up at Dinah from her kneeling position in the straw, there was a small inquisitive crowd in attendance.

'Thrush,' Mercy announced shortly. 'You'll have to treat it every day, morning and evening. Get a stick and sharpen the end of it, not *too* sharp, and pack the cleft of the frog with Stockholm tar and tow. I'll show you how after the ride this morning; there isn't time now. And then you'll have to do it yourself twice a day until it clears up . . . All right, *Yards*, everybody! Yards, please!'

She bounced to her feet, and the watching Horsemasters scattered hastily before her; she charged out to bang on the feed box and shrill, 'Yards, please!' and Dinah, bewildered, asked the others at large:

'What's thrush, anybody remember? We *did* have it. I've got it in my notes, but I just can't seem to –'

'Thrush,' Sally Burnham answered her, 'is an infection of the sensitive frog of the hoof, characterized by an offensive-smelling discharge and a ragged appearance of the frog. It is usually caused' – and Sally's face took on an expression of fiendish glee – 'by dirty stabling, standing in soiled bedding, or the like!'

'Dirty stabling!' Dinah said hotly. 'Now, you look here – I don't care *what* Mr Ffolliott says, Corny P. has the cleanest stall in this place and *I'm* the girl who ought to know! He, by golly, has *not* stood in any soiled bedding, except during the night, and nobody's going to –'

'There are other causes of thrush,' Mercy's high clear

voice cut in coldly, 'and this stable has passed inspection right along. If Cornish Pasty has thrush, it is *not* the fault of his groom. Now will you all get on the yards, please!'

So they got on the yards, without undue resentment, bending their backs in unison to the rhythmic swinging of the heavy brooms and the cascading torrents of cold water until at last the stable yard was a shimmering expanse of clean wet bricks. And then they leaned a moment on their brooms, straightening their aching backs and breathing a little hard, and listening to the welcome sound of the breakfast gong tolling from Allerford House.

'All right, everybody, break –' Mercy began, and in that moment there was a horrible clatter; David and Enzo, scuffling playfully as they put their tools away, had managed to knock over the wheelbarrow, spilling a scant double handful of straw and chaff from the drains to be strewn by the wind over the bricks.

'Breakfast!' Mercy snapped without hesitation, 'for everyone *except* David and Enzo! You two can come up when you've finished sweeping the yard again!'

There was a moment of stunned silence, and Enzo bleated plaintively, as though he could not quite believe in such injustice.

'The *whole* yard?'

'The whole yard!' Mercy snapped, and turned and marched off towards Allerford House, adding over her shoulder, 'The rest of you are dismissed; hurry and change for breakfast.'

But the rest of them did not move, and Mercy's small rigid figure went out of the stable yard alone. Without a word the Horsemasters collected their brooms and buckets again, and savagely attacked the yards all over again. And when they had finished Jill Taylor declared for all of them:

'That snaky little witch makes it so *easy* to hate her! When I think I was actually *worried* about her yesterday, I could kick myself!'

But as they ran up towards Allerford House and the cold unappetizing breakfast that awaited them, a thought flickered into Dinah's mind and got away again before she really had a chance to catch it and examine it: It was, somehow, a kind of relief to be able to hate Mercy again in perfect agreement with everyone else; it bound them all together in a common feeling, made them all *belong* . . .

'With Mr Nicholson as the leading file,' the Major shouted, 'at the M marker, on command, inward turn and halt, form line, rest of the class closing up on Mr Nicholson. All right, Mr Nicholson, inward . . . *tur-r-rn*!'

One after another the trotting horses slowed and obediently turned at right angles to the long wall and halted, facing the opposite wall of the Covered School in a long even line, tossing their heads and mouthing their bits but standing square and steady. The Major surveyed the class briefly, and his frosty blue eyes sparkled with pleasurable anticipation; rubbing his hands together briskly, he said:

'Quite good! That was not bad, not bad at all . . . All right, four of you jump down and bring in two sets of hurdles, four uprights and – ah – six poles. Mr Perrin, Mr Lalli, Mr Nicholson. And you too, Miss Burnham, you look like a strong young lady this morning. Somebody else jump down and hold their horses; smartly, now!'

Dinah slipped out of her saddle and caught Highboy's reins as Enzo, on her left, handed them to her; she stood between Highboy and Night Life patiently holding the two horses as they nuzzled her curiously and then lost interest. Sally and the three boys were running clumsily, their boots sinking into the soft sand and sawdust, to bring in the jumping obstacles from the shed behind the

Covered School; Dinah watched the Major as he stood idly slapping his boot with his stick, his ruddy face displaying vast good humour.

The emphasis had been heavily on jumping during the past two weeks; the Major halted each two-hour ride after one hour's drill at the various gaits, during which he seemed to find less and less fault with the riders, and for the second hour they jumped, singly and in file, over low obstacles. Everyone in the class had had at least one fall this week – Dinah had had three – but no one had been even slightly hurt, and with each day's lesson their confidence grew.

The Major was directing the placement of the hurdles now, one in the middle of each long wall protruding out into the centre of the arena; it seemed to Dinah that he was setting the bars higher than they had been heretofore, and she glanced at Peanuts, who raised an expressive eyebrow and whistled silently. And then the Major was striding back to his place in the centre of the school, commanding:

'All right, mount your horses. Today we shall jump without reins and without stirrups; your seats and your balance and your sense of timing should be good enough by now to keep you all in the plate. You may grab your neck strap if you feel yourself going, but do *not* touch the reins once you have dropped them! You're not to save yourself a fall by pulling on your horse's mouth! All right, Mr Nicholson, will you lead off, please? Trot round – first cross your stirrup leathers over the front of your saddle, that's right; everyone do that, please – trot round to the hurdle at the E marker, drop your reins, fold your arms, and jump it from the trot; continue round to the B marker and jump that from the canter; take up your reins and rejoin the ride. All right, Mr Nicholson, off you go!'

'Quite likely!' Roger said to himself quite audibly, and

a ripple of laughter ran through the school; even the Major, idly slapping his gleaming boot and watching, smiled broadly. Dinah watched, holding her breath, as Bootlegger trotted briskly round the short side of the school, his head high and his neck flexed, and lengthened his stride as he approached the hurdle. And then in the last stride Roger dropped his reins and folded his arms across his chest and bowed forward from the waist as the big horse gathered himself and stretched his neck and jumped. Bootlegger landed running; he cantered hard round the school while Roger, making no effort to touch the reins flapping loose on the horse's neck, sat firmly erect in his saddle; as Bootlegger took off to soar over the second hurdle Roger bent low over the horse's neck again, and on landing recovered the reins and rode quite coolly back to his place.

'Quite!' the Major said with quiet satisfaction. 'That is exactly what I want you all to do. Let me see, who shall we have next? Ah, Miss Wilcox, come and show us the American technique!'

Groaning inwardly, Dinah wheeled Night Life out of line and sent the black mare into a short jogging trot. Her legs, dangling down on either side without stirrups, felt terribly insecure, but at least Night Life was an easy horse to sit and she jumped smoothly and beautifully. And there was the neck-strap . . .

Night Life lengthened her stride and went at the hurdle in a rush; Dinah dropped the reins and folded her arms and as she felt the mare gather her haunches beneath her and surge into the air she bobbed low over Night Life's neck . . . *too late!* She had miscalculated her timing and was not moving with the horse; Night Life was jumping out from under her, leaving Dinah far behind. Desperately she grabbed for the strap at the base of Night Life's neck and got it with both hands; as the mare landed clear and galloped hard round the short side of the school, Dinah clung for dear life. The second hurdle loomed ahead, and she had her balance again now; hurriedly she let go the neck strap and folded her arms, and this time as Night Life jumped Dinah timed it right and stayed with her. But she felt weak and shaken as she recovered her reins and rode back to her place, and worried; after all this time she could *not* anticipate a horse's take-off properly...

'Very good on the second hurdle, Miss Wilcox,' the Major called clearly. 'You were behind your horse over the first, as you know, but it's rather more difficult to jump from the trot ... All right, ah – Miss deMarigny! D'you understand what we're about this morning?'

'Ah, yes!' Adrienne said demurely. 'I am to do as Roger, and not as Dinah, this is so? I will try my best, Major Brooke.'

But Adrienne's best was not good enough; Blue Trout was pulling too hard for her to hold before she even got round the short end of the school; he broke into a wild gallop and soared over the first hurdle while Adrienne clung grimly to the reins and hauled back to no avail; he cleared the second with equal zest and continued on to jump the first again, and showed no sign of slackening his speed as he tore round the school once more, and once again. A month ago the other Horsemasters would have sat still and silent in horrified sympathy; now Dinah was shaking with suppressed giggles, and she could hear muffled laughter all over the school. Even the Major was laughing as Blue Trout, who loved to jump, kept right on jumping; even Adrienne, futilely trying to check the hard-mouthed little roan, looked flustered and exasperated but not by any means frightened.

'All right!' the Major called at last, in a choked voice; he strode briskly to the side of the school and stood in Blue Trout's path as the roan came tearing round. The

Major flapped his hat at Blue Trout, and the roan shied sideways and Adrienne fell off into the sawdust; the Major deftly caught the horse and held him as she got up, brushing at the seat of her jodhpurs.

'I think we'll give Miss deMarigny another horse,' the Major said, 'ah . . . all right, Miss Wilcox, you've had your fun; jump down and give Miss deMarigny Night Life. And now who wants to take the back out of Blue Trout? One of our two undefeated champions . . . all right, Miss Simms, you take Blue Trout round. The first hurdle at the trot and the second at the canter; no reins and no stirrups. And then pull him up and join the ride. Jump down, now; hurry!'

Bee Bye vaulted off Shadow and handed her reins to Enzo to hold; she ran clumsily through the sawdust to the Major, and he gave her a leg up. Blue Trout struck off at a hard trot at once, fighting his head and trying to break into a canter; his blood was up and he saw no reason to stop doing what he was enjoying so much.

'Take him once round the school to get him settled, Miss Simms!' the Major called, and Bee Bye rode the little roan round the school, shying and dancing and throwing his head and kicking; he went sideways more than he went forward, and he would not trot more than a couple of strides before breaking into a canter. Bee Bye, working furiously, got him hauled back to a long, hard extended trot and let him go at the E hurdle fairly straight; as soon as she dropped the reins and folded her arms, however, Blue Trout hurled himself over the hurdle and flattened out, tearing round the school as hard as he could gallop. He soared high and wide over the second hurdle, and Bee Bye grabbed the reins and tried to stop him, but Blue Trout was away again.

The laughter burst out now, and this time it was not muffled; the Major was laughing with the class as Bee Bye, her face drawn in a scowl of concentration, applied all her skill to regain control of the hard-mouthed little run-away. Blue Trout took the first hurdle a second time, and continued; Bee Bye, with her legs closed tight on him, was no longer hauling back hard on the reins but giving and taking rhythmically, taking a firm hold on his mouth and letting it go, and at once taking it again. The little roan sailed over the second hurdle a second time, and per-ceptibly slackened his pace on landing; his head came up and he seemed to be paying attention to the bit, or at least to be aware of it ... and then abruptly his head went down, all the way down between his feet, and he bucked high and hard once, twice, three times.

Bee Bye, riding without stirrups, had no chance to stay in the saddle; she was thrown forward on to Blue Trout's neck by his first mighty buck, and she promptly wound both arms hard round his neck, dropping the reins, and clung like a leech. His second buck loosened her hold a little, and she slipped sideways; his third dislodged her entirely, and she slipped down under his neck. And there she hung, with her arms and legs wound round the little roan's neck, while he stood perfectly still, bewildered.

'She's not off until she touches the ground, y'know!' David's voice rang out above the shrieks of helpless laughter, and suddenly the laughter stopped, or at least subsided to choked and muffled snorts. For Bee Bye, hang-ing upside-down underneath her horse's neck, was not dropping to the ground defeated; she was twisting and straining for leverage to work herself on to his back again.

'That is entirely correct!' the Major said crisply. 'She is not yet off! Persevere, Miss Simms, your record is as yet unsullied! Excelsior!'

The Major turned away, his eyes streaming, and his shoulders shook as the Horsemasters began to call out en-couragement. 'Go *on*, Bee Bye!' 'You can *do* it, Bee Bye!'

'Don't waste your 10p, Bee Bye! The Olympic Team's got plenty of mine!'

And somehow Bee Bye did it. If Blue Trout had moved a muscle, she would have fallen off, but he did not; he stood like a statue, looking as puzzled as a horse can look, and inch by inch Bee Bye struggled round until with one final convulsive effort she heaved herself back on to the roan's neck and lay there limp and panting while the school rang with cheers.

'Well saved, Miss Simms!' the Major congratulated her, when the cheering died away, 'and now I think we'll retire Blue Trout from the lists for today. Mr Perrin, will you take Claddagh Boy round, please?'

But if the Major expected further fireworks, he was doomed to disappointment; Claddagh Boy was in a docile mood, and the rest of the lesson passed without further incident.

'All right,' the Major called at last, 'that will be all for today. Tomorrow you will tack up fifteen minutes early and hack down to the Vale; we are going to be doing our cross-country jumps from now on, one or two each day until we've done them all, and we'll spend tomorrow morning perfecting your timing in the Grid before we start. Class, dis . . . *missed*!'

The tack-room buzzed with excited, incoherent conversation; there were two bridles on every hook and a saddle on every sawhorse, and as everyone scrubbed fiercely away with damp cloths and saddle soap and metal polish, they were all talking at once.

'Did you *hear* what he said?' Peanuts demanded excitedly, and Dinah answered glumly.

'Did I hear what he said? I can *still* hear him saying it! Tomorrow the Grid, that's what he said. Smiling and happy and obviously enjoying the prospect, without a thought for my poor parents sorrowing in their bereavement ... Peanuts, I think I am going to be sick!'

'Not in here, you're not!' Betsy Murphy said sharply. 'I'm cleaning the tack-room this week! Go and be sick outside somewhere. Go and be sick in the Covered School!'

'No!' Jill yelped. 'Not there! Anywhere but there! Roger and I are raking the school this week; it's bad enough without cleaning up after you, Wilcox!'

'My *friends*!' Dinah muttered dolefully. 'I'm about to die of fright, and all they can do is argue about who has to bury the body! Isn't *anybody* scared of that horrible thing but me?'

'Oh, it isn't the cough that carries you off, it's the coffin they carry you off in!' David chanted happily. 'And it isn't the Grid – let me see ... Oh, it isn't the Grid that'll ruin you, kid; it's the fences where real accidents is! ... *Hey*, how d'you like that! Perrin, the Poet Laureate!'

'Shocking poetry, but rather good sense,' Sally said. 'It *isn't* the Grid you have to worry about, Dinah, it's what he said comes later. The cross-country jumps. Have you *seen* 'em?'

'I've seen some of them,' Dinah said, 'the fence thing in the upper paddock, and the hole in the ground with the fences on both sides. Do we have to jump *those*? Oh, not *really*?'

'We do, though, y'know,' Roger told her quietly, 'we have to jump everything on the course. And there are some obstacles that look a lot worse than the pen and the ditch-and-rails, too. But thirty-some Horsemastership classes have got through this place before us, so I dare say we'll muddle through somehow without actually getting killed. Want to walk over the whole course after lunch, and look 'em all over?'

'Oh, I say, *let's*!' Peanuts cried enthusiastically, and Bee Bye said at once:

'*I'd* like to; I haven't any idea what lies ahead, and I'd like to have an inkling before the Major springs it on us. He had entirely too much fun with me this morning!'

'He doesn't half enjoy bashing us about, doesn't he?' Roger agreed, laughing. 'But, d'you notice, he not only acts as though he's enjoying himself now, as we come hurtling off and grimly scramble back aboard again, he's beginning to act as though he *likes* us?'

'I think he is proud of us,' Adrienne said unexpectedly, 'all of us, even me. And me, I feel the same; if the Major led out a sabre-toothed tiger with a saddle on it and said, "Mount this, Miss deMarigny!" I would mount it. I do not know why, exactly, because I would be afraid; I am afraid even of Blue Trout, who always runs away with me; but I would think "*Eh bien*, the Major thinks I can, and so I must try or he will be not proud of me!" And I would try.'

There was a long and profoundly thoughtful silence, and then David said quietly:

'D'you know, I think this is getting to be a jolly good group to be a part of!'

And Dinah thought, Why, that's right! We'll *all* do the Grid, and it won't be any worse for me than for any of the others; I don't think I really mind at all ...

And then a crashing note of discord shattered the moment of revelation; Mercy's shrill voice crying metallically:

'All right, everybody, yards, please; *yards*, everybody!'

Chapter 9

Less Than Three Weeks

Shadow came rocketing out of the grid and Enzo, tight in the saddle, whooped exuberantly and caught up his reins and turned the horse, riding her back to the end of the waiting line with a wide, delighted smile on his face. And then Sally was riding Cotton Socks into the starting end, drumming his sides with her heels and urging him on with voice and body, and Dinah thought, *Ouch, I'm next!*

She felt suddenly small and alone, perched high in the middle of Pipe Clay's broad white back; she was in fact alone, for Toni Harper on her left was keeping a prudent interval between Nutmeg and Pipe Clay's dreaded, great yellow teeth. Enzo was excitedly telling Betsy Murphy all about it, waving his arms in wild gesticulations as he talked excitedly; Enzo looked as though he had really enjoyed it. And Ingrid and Peanuts and Gretel, who had gone before Enzo, had all emerged looking flushed and excited and somehow exhilarated. But it still looked formidable to –

Sally had got Cotton Socks turned round and dropped her reins, and he was stubbornly refusing to approach the first cross-pole; Sally was drumming her heels into his sides and screaming vehemently, 'Go *on, go on*; Cotton Socks, you horrible horse, *GO ON!*' And then Cotton Socks, who positively hated jumping, resignedly took a step forward. He eyed the cross-pole suspiciously, while Sally continued to kick and belabour him and shriek in his ear, and twitched his haunches delicately like a fat woman in a tight corset to get his hocks under him; then he reluctantly hopped over the first pole.

This brought him face to face with the second cross-pole, and Cotton Socks stopped dead and sized-up the situation. He had just jumped over a pole like this, reluctantly and against his better judgement, because this fool girl on his back had made such a fuss about it, and now look where it had got him! There was another pole just like it, and beyond this one there were others, a whole long row of 'em. On the other hand, there wasn't room to turn round and go back, and the rider on his back was still kicking his sides rudely and violently, and that whole crowd of people outside looking on were shrieking and laughing and making an intolerable racket.

Resignedly, Cotton Socks tucked his hocks up under him again and jumped the next bar; he kept right on bouncing over one after another until he emerged from the other end of the Grid, and everyone cheered gaily as he turned in response to the rein and trotted back to the end of the line with his head proudly high.

Dinah rode Pipe Clay forward without hesitation; the huge mare turned round with difficulty in the confined space at the end of the Grid, and Dinah dropped her reins and folded her arms and rocked forward as Pipe Clay surged forward and up over the first bar. And then, as the big mare went bounding down the row of cross-poles, the motion of her surging upward and coming down and surging up again rocked Dinah's body back and forth rhythmically; she realized all at once that she was moving exactly in time with Pipe Clay's movements, and that she was secure in the saddle without reins or stirrups as she had never felt secure while jumping before!

Pipe Clay came over the last cross-pole and out into the flat; Dinah reached for the reins and brought the big mare round and back to the waiting line. She could feel the blood pounding in her veins and her cheeks stiff with the width of her delighted grin; she felt like whooping as Enzo had whooped. So that was the Grid! It was *fun*, and she was already impatient for her turn to come again; further, its purpose was plain enough now. She could still feel it, that exact moment when Pipe Clay's quarters gathered under her to launch the big mare into the air; a few more times down the Grid and she would know the feeling so well she would know the movement for evermore, the moment to rock her body with a horse taking off for a jump.

Jill stretched on tiptoe, balancing Shadow's gleaming saddle on her head with a hand beneath it on either side, and with a mighty effort heaved it on to its rack. She then clambered up on to a chair and attached the stirrup leathers, running the stirrup irons up snugly against the bar, and jumped down heavily.

'That's *my* tack finished for today,' she announced, 'anyone else need help? Anyone on Blue Ride, that is? What's the time, anyway?'

'It is . . .' Enzo answered, pulling out a gold pocket watch and peering at it closely, 'it is twenty-two minutes past two hours. We have eight minutes before lecture; six minutes here if we run all the way to the Blue Room. And I will run; I have still much work to do!'

'Ye dinna hae t'hurry, then,' Jock Woods called from the tack-room doorway, and they all turned as the Stud Groom sauntered in, grinning amiably, and tossed his cap on to the bench beneath the window and hoisted himself to sit with his legs dangling.

'Mr Ffolliott will nae be lecturin' the day,' Jock told them all, still grinning, 'ye'll hae m'self in his place. An' since I canna gie a proper lecture wi' notes an' all, we needna go to the Blue Room. Ye can continue wi' your workin' on your tack, an' I'll gie ye all a little talk an' perhaps a little quiz. 'Tis a quiz, by the way, that Mr Ffolliott is preparin' for you lot today; he'll gie it ye the morrow.'

'A *quiz!*' three or four voices groaned together in dismay and disgust. 'What for?'

'Ye'll be havin' 'em three times a week from now on,' Jock said soberly, 'all made up from questions the B.H.S. Examiner has put in the Written Examination other years. An' since ye ask, I'll tell ye what for: because 'tis less than three weeks until the Examiner comes, that's what for! Three weeks from today ye'll be all finished here – and in some ways ye've hardly got started! Oh, you're a bright bunch, all right; an' your ridin's not near so bad as it was; you *might* even pass the ridin' part of the Exam, if the Major can teach ye to handle the cross-country course in th' next two weeks. But can ye sit here an' pass the General Knowledge questions the Examiner will ask ye? And can ye take the Written Exam on Minor Ailments an' Stable Management an' that lot?'

Only three weeks! Dinah thought, *It isn't possible!* But she looked from Peanuts's startled, sobered face to Bee Bye's to Toni's, and so round the room; peering through bridles and over saddles, all the solemn eyes were fixed on Jock, soapy sponges dripped, forgotten in limp hands, on the red-tiled floor ...

'Supposin', then,' Jock said softly, 'that the Examiner were sittin' here; supposin' he asked ye what would ye say was wrong wi' a horse that ye found lyin' down in his box, maybe tryin' to roll, then gettin' up an' movin' all round his box, kickin' at his belly, maybe breakin' out in a sweat ... Peanuts? ... Ingrid? ... Adrienne?'

'He has *mal*, here,' Adrienne said, patting her stomach. 'I do not remember the name, a pain in the – ah, it is *colic!*'

'Colic,' Jock said, nodding, 'right-o. All right, it's your

horse, Dinah. What are you going to do about it?'

Desperately Dinah searched her memory; she could recall Mr Ffolliott reciting a list of things to do in the case
of a horse with stomach ache, but all that came back to
her was –

'Give him a colic drench?' she suggested, and Jock's grin
broadened. Looking as though he were enjoying himself
hugely, he fixed his twinkling eyes on Dinah's and softly
inquired:

'How?'

Turpentine and whisky and linseed oil, Dinah's mind
chanted derisively, turpentine and whisky and linseed oil.
And what in the *world* do you do with it? Put it in a
bucket and feed it to him? I bet no horse alive would
drink a mixture like that! And how would you go about
making him drink it ... ?

Helplessly, she shook her head, and Jock glanced round
the room and nodded, and hopped down from his perch.

'Old Roger, here, he's a farm boy, so he's given a horse a
drench in his day,' Jock said cheerfully. 'Any o' the rest o'
ye think ye know how? No? All right, then, let's go give a
horse a drench. The Examiner made one o' my lot do it,
two years back; she didn't half make a mess of it! Come
on, the lot of ye!'

He opened the door of Mercy's medicine chest, in the
corner, and took down a tall, slim tapering bottle and a
strip of cloth from the top shelf; the Horsemasters put
down their sponges and polishing cloths and followed him
as he led the way out into the stable yard and filled the
bottle from the tap.

'A little drink o' water willna hurt th' horse,' Jock said
cheerfully, 'but it may be a mite damp for Roger an' me
... anyone got a couple ridin' macs down here?'

There were half a dozen old riding macs in the closet
behind the tack-room; Dinah, being nearest the door,

hurried in and grabbed two, and Jock and Roger each donned one.

'All right,' Jock said cheerfully, 'now we need a horse.'

'Use Pipe Clay!' Peanuts urged, and Jock bent a knowing eye on the jaunty little girl and answered:

'So 'twould amuse ye to see me lose my arm, would it now, ye little imp? Well, 'tis not in the lesson for today – but I'll hae a lesson for *you* one day! No, we'll hae a nice quiet horse that doesna bite ... ah, there's old Cornish Pasty, he'll do us! Who's groom for Cornish Pasty? You, Dinah? Well, untie your horse an' turn him round in his stall so he's facin' out ...'

Rather reluctantly Dinah slipped into Corny P.'s stall and went to his head, patting his inquisitive nose as she untied the weight from his rope and pulled the rope through the ring on the wall, and led him carefully round to face out of the stall. Jock wasn't going to *hurt* him, of course; still she wished someone else's horse might have been selected to submit to the indignity of being used for a demonstration in the middle of the afternoon; it seemed a pity and an imposition to disturb poor old Corny in the middle of his rest period.

'This is a hock bottle,' Jock said, holding up the long, tapering wine bottle, 'and it makes the best bottle there is for givin' a drench, because of the shape – there's no shoulders to it. Now, we wrap the neck of the bottle in a cloth so's it won't rattle against his back teeth an' maybe break in his mouth, an' then the next thing is to get him to drink from it. First we slip the end of the neck in his mouth, like this ...'

The bottle's slim neck went into Corny P.'s mouth easily enough, but Corny promptly bent his neck and dropped his head; it was quite clear that he did not intend to drink from it.

'An' now,' Jock said cheerfully, 'since a liquid will nae

flow *up* his throat, we must get his head up. *High* up.
Roger!'

Roger stepped forward; he had a pitchfork in his hand.
He deftly twisted the handle firmly into Corny's stall
collar, seized the base close to the tines in both hands, and
with one swift heave forced Corny's head high above his
own, and held it there. Corny P., with his chin pointing
skyward rolled a distressed and questioning eye sideways
and down at Dinah; the wrapped hock bottle was still in
his mouth, however, and now Jock extended his arm as
high as he could and tipped it up, and the water gurgled
out of it into the horse's throat.

Well ... *some* of it was going down Corny's throat, because Dinah could see him swallowing. But he was
struggling, jerking his head as best he could against
Roger's hold and Jock's, which wasn't much; it was
enough, though, to spray water all over the two of them
and make the watching Horsemasters step back a little.
And then Jock withdrew the bottle and Roger withdrew
his pitchfork, and Corny P. dropped his head and shook it
hard, blowing through his nostrils as Jock and Roger
stepped back and began divesting themselves of their
riding macs.

'An' that,' Jock said, 'is how you give a horse a drench.
Ye'll use the same system to give him a ball, but wi' one
difference: a horse can take his pill an' stand lookin' ye
right in the eye all day long, an' when ye muck him out in
the mornin' ye'll find the ball right where he spit it out as
soon as ye left. So ye hold his head up an' put the ball as
far back in his mouth as ye can, an' then ye gie him a little
chop right across the Adam's apple wi' th' side o' your
hand, an' he'll gie a convulsive little gulp an' swallow it
... All right, Dinah, this is your horse – show us how ye'd
go about getting him to open his mouth *and hold it open*
the while ye had a good look at his teeth or whatever.'

Dinah hesitated, puzzled; then she took Corny's nose in one hand and his jaw in the other and slipped her thumb into the corner of his mouth, and he opened it. But he pulled away, turning his head, and she could not hold him still; she tried again with the same result, and again . . .

'All right, Dinah,' Jock said quietly. 'Now put your hand to the side o' his mouth wi' your pinky against the corner of it, an' slide your whole hand in wi' your four fingers flat on top of his tongue an' your thumb underneath it. An' take a nice firm hold o' his tongue – ye'll not hurt him – an' turn it up against the roof of his mouth . . . *so!* Now he'll stand there wi' his mouth wide open for as long as ye want him to, an' quiet; he's not about to pull at his own tongue! All right, ye can let him go now, Dinah.'

Dinah released Corny P., who snorted again but did not appear to be at all distressed, really, and absently wiped her hand on the seat of her jeans. This was *interesting*, she thought; it was much more interesting to learn something by doing it than just by listening to Mr Ffolliott drone along and writing everything down in a notebook. And you learned *how* to give a drench this way, or –

'Now, the Examiner is surely goin' to ask you a question about shoein',' Jock said quietly, 'for the most important part of a horse is his feet. No foot, no 'oss. So we'll just hae a look at some different shoes on different horses here, startin' wi' old Corny since we're visitin' him . . . *Hello,* what's this? Thrush?'

He had picked up Corny P.'s near hind as the Horsemasters crowded close round him, and now he turned his head to give Dinah an inquiring look and she nodded and said:

'Yes. I've been packing it with Stockholm tar and tow twice a day; it's almost gone now.'

'Comin' along fine,' Jock concurred. 'All right, now who can describe this shoe? Sally?'

'It looks like an ordinary hunting shoe,' Sally responded briskly, 'it's fullered and seated out, and aside from that it's –'

'*Wuh*-ho-o!' Jock interrupted. 'Everybody understand what Sally's talking about? No? All right – a shoe with a groove all round, like this, and the nails placed in the groove is a *fullered* shoe. The groove lightens the weight of the shoe; it also keeps the nail heads countersunk out of the way. A *seated-out* shoe has a bevelled inner edge, like this, which also lightens the weight and reduces th' risk of the horse over-reaching an' kickin' himself in the foreleg when galloping. All right, we'll go look at somebody else's shoes; tie up your horse an' come along, Dinah!'

The cavernous empty Covered School was a vast expanse of dark-brown, freshly moistened sand and sawdust rippled and pocked with hoof marks; all the way round the vast arena, close to the walls, ran the deep depression of the track where the horses had circled during the day, their hooves throwing sand and sawdust aside, mounding it against the boards.

Bee Bye was dragging the hose outside; the watering was finished, the footing was moist enough not to throw up clouds of dust during tomorrow's ride. Sighing, Dinah squared her shoulders and picked up a shovel; bending, she began the long, long journey round the walls, shovelling the mounded sand and sawdust back into the depression of the track and levelling it off. Behind her she heard Bee Bye return, heard the chink and scrape of Bee Bye's shovel working round the other side of the school to meet her. This was certainly the hardest of the 'extra chores' that Mercy assigned to the Horsemasters for a week at a time; during her supposedly free hour between haying up and dinner Dinah had been teamed with Peanuts to polish all the brasses in the yards and stables every day for one week, and with Roger to tidy up the tack-room and scrub its floor every day for another week, and with –

The chink and scrape of Bee Bye's shovel was quite close now, and Dinah shovelled a little faster; now she could see Bee Bye out of the corner of her eye, and the unfinished strip grew shorter and shorter until Bee Bye's shovel beat her own to the last shovelful of sawdust and threw it into the last shallow depression of the track, and Dinah straightened her aching back and leaned on the handle of her shovel to face her friend. She was flushed and breathing hard, and so was Bee Bye; for a moment they rested, and then Dinah murmured:

'Three *weeks*, Bee Bye! *Less* than three weeks! And I don't know a *thing*!'

'I certainly don't feel like taking any General Knowledge examination, myself,' Bee Bye said firmly, 'nor any so-called Minor Ailments one, either. Though I wish we could have more sessions with Jock like that one this afternoon. I bet we'd learn a lot in a hurry. And practical stuff, too.'

'Well, we couldn't very well get a lot of the things Mr Ffolliott gives us in the notes,' Dinah argued sensibly, 'because a lot of it's injuries and diseases and symptoms and treatments ... But it *was* a fascinating afternoon, and not so confusing as the lectures. Darn it, I *can't* keep straight in my head all the things I've written down but don't really understand; when you *see* something like the different kinds of shoes, it's easier to remember what they look like and what they're for. But we have to know all that stuff in the notes, too, Bee Bye.'

'From now on,' Bee Bye said, and solemnly raised her

hand, 'I swear to study *every* night. And *hard*. Okay, now let's get this horrible place raked.'

Together they marched, with their shovels on their shoulders like rifles, to the door and out and round the corner to exchange the shovels for two broad heavy iron rakes; together they marched back again and, leaning far forward like a pair of straining plough horses, dragged the heavy rakes from one end of the arena to the other and turned and dragged them back again. And turned, and laboured the length of the arena again, and again, and again.

They finished finally, at the door and turned to survey the vast area of dark brown combed with neat parallel rows of sharp lines gently undulating, and Dinah wiped perspiration from her brow, and said:

'*Whew!* Well, I guess that does it, huh?'

'I don't know,' Bee Bye said dubiously. 'Look up there at the end, in the far corner beyond the K marker ... it isn't level, y'know. *Definitely* a hollow!'

'Not *much* of a hollow!' Dinah protested, and groaned, 'Oh, *don't* say we have to do it again! Surely that's good enough!'

'Maybe,' Bee Bye murmured dubiously, '*maybe* it's good enough; it isn't *much* of a hollow. But just two weeks from today are the Hunter Trials, and we lead Red Ride by about fifteen demerits as of this morning. Think we ought to risk five for School Not Properly Raked?'

'Mercy hasn't been handing 'em out so freely lately,' Dinah said hopefully, eyeing the enormous expanse of sand and sawdust with distaste, 'maybe ...'

'Only because she hasn't been able to find much to hand 'em out *for*,' Bee Bye said firmly, 'and you know it! She's still looking as hard as ever, and she still doesn't miss much; it's just that there isn't much to miss. If I do say it myself, we're getting pretty darned good, all of us; I've *never* seen stables kept the way we're keeping these. And boy, am I going to be a holy terror to my father's grooms when I get home!'

'Considering the tools they give us to work with,' Dinah agreed, 'we *are* doing quite a job, aren't we? If they'd provide enough brooms to go round, nice new brooms with bristles in 'em, it would be a lot easier, but even as it is we must be doing pretty well if even Mercy can't fault the stables very often ... Oh, come on, we might as well rake the flaming place all over again, that little old hollow is beginning to make *me* feel dissatisfied!'

Chapter 10

The Cross-country Course

'Oh, boy!' Peanuts said sunnily, digging into a heaping bowl of cornflakes, 'Saturday morning! And a lovely sunny one at that; we shall have a wonderful hack! Pass the sugar, will you please, Dinah?'

'And no more lessons until Monday,' Ingrid added as Dinah reached for the sugarbowl and slid it along the polished wood of the long table to Peanuts. 'I think this, too, is pleasant to contemplate, not? It is nothing to worry all day today, all day tomorrow!'

'Ah,' Adrienne murmured softly, smiling, 'but the very best of *all* is that it is our week-end off, Blue Ride! It will be from just now forty-five hours and twenty minutes before we must arise and go to muck out stables again, I am keeping count ... Will anyone have more tea?'

'I'll *bet* you're keeping count, Sleepy!' David said as everyone laughed at Adrienne, 'and I bet we shall know where to find you all day tomorrow while Red Ride toils in the stables piling up masses of demerits!'

'And this afternoon as well,' Adrienne murmured, nodding, 'I shall be in bed. But please, unless the house is afire, do not come to find me – and not then unless the firemen have given up all hope!'

'Red Ride has not had a demerit since Wednesday,' Enzo said soberly, rising and gathering up his empty bowl and Gretel's, 'and we will not acquire any more this week-end, nor after. Next week is the Hunter Trials, and we have already bought our tickets!'

Red Ride cheered lustily, and Blue Ride jeered. We *are*

a serenely happy-looking bunch this morning! Dinah
thought. And not much wonder, with the week over and a
morning ahead, and only one more week of classes to go
... oh – oh, the List!

Mercy was standing up, banging on a glass with a fork,
and gradually the hubbub quietened, and one by one the
Horsemasters turned their attention to the Head Girl. But
Mercy's hands were empty when she put down the fork;
instead of reading from the List as usual she announced in
her high clear voice:

'There isn't any List this morning. You will all ride
your own horses. And instead of a hack, you're all going
to do the cross-country course – one at a time, over
the –'

'The *cross-country course*!' Sally shrieked, incredulous,
'You mean the whole *thing*? Oh, my achin' back – we shall
all be killed!'

They were all yelling excitedly, protesting and dis-
believing and joyous all at the same time; Mercy pounded
frantically on the table and finally got their attention
again, and continued without emotion.

'You will be sent off one at a time at one-minute intervals,' she said coldly, 'and you will ride the course the
Major has laid out for you, non-stop. The course is two
and a half miles long, and there are exactly twenty-five
jumps. You will find –'

Her thin voice was lost in the resurgent racket again,
and she stopped talking and simply stood there at the head
of the table, pale and emotionless, and waited. The bottom seemed to have dropped out of Dinah's stomach; she
felt completely empty. *We've had all the jumps in the
cross-country course*, she reminded herself desperately,
not all at once, but –

But the all-gone feeling persisted: some of them were
terrifying even when you waited your turn and then rode

at one with the rest of the class sitting their horses silently encouraging you on –

'You will find,' Mercy said levelly, 'that it's far easier, actually, to go the whole course at a good hunting pace than it is to take the jumps separately, as you've been doing, in cold blood. Now, the Major will meet you all at the stables to walk the course in fifteen minutes; you can tack up when you get back and you will ride at ten-thirty. That's all.'

She sat down and reached for her teacup, quite unconcerned, as the hubbub broke out again. Peanuts looked a little green, Dinah observed, but it didn't make her feel much better; Bee Bye nudged her sharply and inquired, grinning:

'What's the matter, Dinah, girl? You don't look entirely happy. Something you ate?'

'I feel,' Dinah answered wanly, 'as though all the sawdust just ran out of me. Limp. Completely. Oh, Bee Bye!'

Jill Taylor reached out across the table and lifted the cover off the big platter and yelped:

'Bacon and eggs! Anyone not want theirs!'

Peanuts jumped up and gave Jill one horrified look and fled; Dinah pushed her chair back and stood up rather shakily. She said faintly:

'Peanuts doesn't. And neither do I. And I don't see how even *you* can, Jill! I don't think I *ever* want to see food again!'

'The condemned,' Jill told her, grinning happily and helping herself to three eggs and a mountain of fat bacon, 'always eat a hearty breakfast! Anyone else not want theirs?'

The Major strode purposefully through the lush green grass of the show-jumping paddock, slapping his boots with his stick, and the Horsemasters trailed after him in a ragged group. The Major stopped, and they crowded closer round him.

'You'll start here,' he began crisply, and pointed with his stick, 'and jump the stile. That'll be Number One, the stile.'

'And having left a knee on either post,' Sally whispered, staring at the narrow stile in round-eyed horror, 'keeping the legless torso somehow upright in the saddle, we continue – to what?'

'Oh, shut *up*, Sally!' Toni Harper urged, and they all moved off close after the Major, who nimbly climbed over the stile and continued a few paces before halting at a row of hay bales.

'Number Two,' he remarked laconically, tapping the bales with his stick, and climbed over them and continued. At least, Dinah thought, Number Two doesn't look so bad – if I get over the stile. I *wish* Sally hadn't said that; it *is* hideously narrow.

'Number Three,' the Major announced, 'will be the drop fence, here, into this paddock. You will then continue to take the fallen tree, there – and go at that at a good pace. It's a big jump, as some of you may remember. Then circle wide round and have this drop over the ditch into the lower paddock.'

He marched off briskly through the high white gate into the lower paddock, while Dinah thought, *I* remember that fallen tree, all right! She shuddered, recalling how Highboy had refused it three times and then had had a half-hearted try at it, hitting it hard and only just barely managing not to fall with her. It was a horribly solid-looking tree trunk, too.

'You'll circle wide round here,' the Major said, sweeping his stick round, 'and come on again at a good pace, and have the Piano for Number, ah, Number Six . . .'

There was a dismayed murmur as the Major climbed

briskly up over the Piano, a pair of distressingly solid
three-foot-six-inch earth-and-timber banks set one over the
other like two giant steps. But they scrambled doggedly
after him, and the Major stopped and turned and faced
them all with a smile, and said cheerfully:

'And Number Seven will be the Coffin!'

This time they groaned aloud, in chorus, and Peanuts
whispered:

'I feel faint! I mean, positively *faint*!'

'Me, too,' Dinah whispered back, staring unhappily at
the treacherous, steep gravelly slide with the deep ditch
like an open grave at its bottom and the fiendish oak post-
and-rails sticking up from the middle of the ditch. She
could remember, all too vividly, how it had felt to be on
Shadow's back as she slithered helplessly down the steep
incline with all four feet braced in a vain attempt to stop
herself, and then at the last moment before falling into the
open grave to break her legs on the oak rail had somehow
jumped clear of the thing and stumbled and recovered,
and galloped off. Had somebody actually cleared that
thing on old Corny P.? Or hadn't he been on the ride that
day? She couldn't remember seeing him jump the Coffin
... *could* the old horse do it?

'Number Eight will be the ditch and bank into the
upper paddock again,' the Major announced, 'and then
you will try to check your pace a little as you take that
little white fence into the wood. The path in the wood is
rather narrow, and as you may recall there are three fences
set at rather awkward angles behind the market garden;
if you go at this bit a little too fast you may find yourself
hanging in the trees like ripe fruit ... The little white
fence will be Number Nine; then you will have Ten,
Eleven, and Twelve along the winding path behind the
market garden, and that brings us to the Park Bench –'

Lugubriously they trailed along, while the Major waxed

more and more merry as he led them past jump after jump, numbering each and counselling how and at what pace to approach it. The Park Bench stood under an enormous tree, and riders of tall horses who jumped big would do well to duck low beneath the overhanging limb. The double brush fence was an in-and-out, with room for a horse to take a single stride between the two jumps; check him and go at it slowly, or he'd take you through the second one. The water jump over the brook wasn't as tricky as it looked, with that downhill take-off, but there was rather a sharp turn to be made on landing, and the landing area might get a bit poached by the time the last horses got to it.

'If the first ones get this far,' Jill whispered behind Dinah, 'let alone the last ones ... I'm beginning to wish I'd left that fourth egg and bacon!'

Dinah checked Corny P.'s bridle once again, just to make absolutely sure it was properly adjusted with the bit snug in the corners of his mouth but not tight enough to wrinkle the skin; it was. She stepped back and strained to cinch up his girth one more hole; this would be no day to have the saddle slip. Dolefully, she did not see how she had a chance in the world of getting round that course on old Corny P. Not that she would have had *much* chance on any other horse, of course; but poor old Corny with his shambling disjointed gaits –

She patted his neck consolingly, thinking with a little lift that at least he wouldn't do anything to hurt her; she knew him so well, after all these weeks of practically living in his stall with him, that it was impossible to feel any alarm at the prospect of riding Corny anywhere. It occurred to her that that was probably just why they had all been assigned to the horses with which they were most familiar, to give them that small feeling of confidence; if so, she decided, it was intelligent planning on the Major's part. But she would still prefer to be riding Nightingale, who jumped like a stag, or possibly –

'All right, file out, everybody!' Mercy shrilled from the stable yard. 'Lead your horses into the show-jumping paddock and mount, and then trot and canter round the paddock for fifteen minutes to warm them up. And *don't* forget to check your girths after the first five minutes! All right, file out!'

'And wait till you see what's going on outside!' Roger said gleefully as Dinah led Corny P. in a lazy shuffling walk past Copper. 'This might have come as a surprise to *us*, but not to anyone else in the Vale. Half England's lined up round the course to watch the sport and cheer us on – or off! I *think* they must expect off; there's even an ambulance parked up at the end of the top paddock!'

'There's *always* an ambulance present at Hunter Trials or Point-to-Points or Cross-Country events, and you know it, Roger Nicholson!' Mercy Hale snapped coldly. 'Now you just stop trying to terrify everybody else, and get your horse out there!'

But there *was* an ambulance parked in the top paddock; worse, there were two stretchers laid out on the grass beside it, and two businesslike-looking men in uniform standing close by. Dinah's stomach began doing nip-ups again as she led Corny P. down the lane to the open gate of the show-jumping paddock.

And there *was* a crowd, too. There were thirty or forty strangers clustered near the open gate, watching as the horses were led into the paddock, and she could see little groups of three or four walking in the paddocks beyond, evidently choosing spots along the course from which to watch the riders as they came past.

'We shall do the same next week at the Hunter Trials,' David told her, smiling pleasantly; just to observe David's perfect coolness made Dinah feel a little less uneasy. 'Watch three or four horses over one jump, you know, and then cut across the course to watch one or two others over another, and so on. Of course, one tries to decide in advance which will be the most difficult jumps, so as not to miss anything . . .'

'Such as a nice spectacular fall,' Dinah nodded and to her own vast surprise giggled. David looked at her in surprise, and then smiled warmly.

'Which you won't have with old Corny P., you know,' he told her, and added, 'y'know, I thought you were nervous, Dinah. And I'm *very* glad to find you're not. Good show! Actually, you're going to enjoy this, y'know; it's only the getting ready that's rather hard on one's nerves. Well, let's mount and trot about a bit, shall we?'

Not much I'm not nervous! Dinah thought; but she was not so much so as she had been. Rising rhythmically to ease the jar of Corny's appalling trot, she began to feel a pleasurable tingle of excitement, a reckless readiness to get on with it. She put Corny into a canter, and at once he stretched his neck and took a hard pull at his bit, straining to get into a hard gallop. Corny felt it, too, that reckless excitement, that tingling eagerness to go; perhaps she had communicated the feeling to him. At any rate he was now communicating it to her; she forgot her doubts that the old horse was capable of negotiating the Major's course without mishap, and let him out another notch, cantering fast round the big paddock with zestful abandon.

And then the Major was striding into the centre of the paddock, waving his stick; obediently Dinah hauled Corny P. down and trotted in to sit her horse in a row with the others facing the Major. Now, all at once, she was again aware of the spectators; they had all left the paddock gate now, but she could see little groups of them far off in the distant paddocks, one little knot of people by the

Coffin, another just climbing over the white fence to disappear into the wood . . .

'Check your girths,' the Major said quietly, and guiltily Dinah reached down to check her girth, and then stuck her leg out while she pulled up the cinch two holes.

'Now, we'll send you off one at a time,' the Major said in a comfortable conversational tone, 'at one-minute intervals, so if anyone gets into any trouble please *get off the course at once*, out of the way of the horses following. Captain Pinski and Jock Woods and Mr Ffolliott and Mercy are all spotted round the course at strategic points to help anyone in difficulty or signal you to slow down if there is any, ah, obstruction ahead.'

'Such as bodies strewn about,' somebody said audibly from down the line, but no one laughed.

'Now, I want to send the fast horses off first,' the Major went on, 'to minimize the inconvenience of your catching up with one another. So this will be the order of your departure. Listen carefully, please: Bay Rum will go first, then Mayfly second, then Pennant third, then Nightingale fourth, then Cornish Pasty fifth, then –'

'*What?*' Dinah blurted before she could stop herself, and the Major checked himself and his gay white smile flashed in his lean ruddy face as he told her dryly:

'You will find Cornish Pasty quite a different horse over a cross-country course, Miss Wilcox. That horse was born to hounds; hunting is the one thing he knows, and going across country is the thing he loves best. Just try not to run down those ahead of you if you can avoid it, please. Now, Copper will go sixth, and Claddagh Boy – my *word*! You've switched with Mr Perrin. You were to ride your regular horses. I can't delay much now. Are you sure you can handle Claddagh Boy, Miss Harper? He can be difficult, you know. Perhaps you'd better change with Mr Perrin again. I really don't –'

'Oh, no, *please*, Major Brooke!' Toni begged tensely. '*Please* let me ride him; I *do* want to!'

'All right,' the Major said after a moment, and went on with his list. He finished it and then added: 'Well. That's that. Is everyone ready? Well, Mr Perrin on Bay Rum – *away!*'

Bay Rum snorted, and dark-brown clods spurted from beneath his hooves as he thundered at the narrow stile and jumped, and for an instant seemed to fill it completely, and then was gone to reappear momentarily beyond the hedge as he rose to soar over the bales. He disappeared again, leaving behind him only the thrilling thunder of his hooves and a faint thin cloud of dust hanging in the air beyond the stile.

'Hold them *straight* at the stile,' the Major called crisply, 'it's narrow, you know!' He looked down at his watch and waited, and then commanded:

'All right, Mayfly; off you go, Miss Gotwals!'

Gretel went off more slowly, holding Mayfly to a canter approaching the stile; the mare was pulling eagerly, however, and the beat of her hooves accelerated suddenly after she cleared the stile; she went at the bales in a rush, and was gone.

'All right, Pennant!' the Major called. And then a minute later, 'All right, Nightingale!' and Sally gave Dinah a great derisive wink that said *don't you wish you had this horse instead of that clumsy old plug!* and was gone, howling, in a series of great stag-like leaps.

It's funny, Dinah thought, I'm next; it's practically my turn right this instant, and I'm not nervous. *Nobody's* nervous any more; nobody's scared. Toni Harper's riding Claddagh Boy; she's never even been *on* him before. And I'm –

'All right, Cornish Pasty!' the Major called sharply, and Corny P. practically shot out from under Dinah in his eagerness to respond to her spur. The stile rushed at her, and Corny surged upwards under her and instinctively her body rocked with his; then came the jar of landing and the bales were ahead and beneath and behind. There was no sound in all the world but the frantic hammering of his hooves; the wind was blasting at her face and the drop fence rushed at her and Dinah thought *I can't hold him, he's running away with me. I've never gone so fast on a horse before.*

Corny catapulted over the drop and landed heavily, but he did not miss a stride; he thundered on and cleared the fallen tree in a prodigious leap before Dinah had really had time to feel apprehensive about it. She hauled hard on the reins and Corny did not check his speed one whit, but he did swerve obediently, and she brought him round in a sweeping circle and aimed him, still going at his all-out gallop, at the drop over the ditch. She knew now that she couldn't slow him, and didn't seem to care; she could steer him all right and she didn't *want* to go slower.

They cleared the ditch by a wide margin, but the drop was a big one; the jar of landing threw Dinah forward off-balance and she nearly went off. But she recovered herself and brought Corny round in a wide swing to approach the Piano at his fastest clip. But there was another horse there! It was Nightingale, prancing and dancing and shying away and obstinately refusing to have any part of those formidable-looking banks, while Sally kicked him and whipped him and yelled at him, looking fearfully over her shoulder at the approaching thunder of Corny P.

Dinah yelled at the top of her lungs and kept coming, and Sally jumped Nightingale out of the way. As Corny pounded past, Dinah yelled at Sally, 'Get a *horse*!' Then Corny P. bounded up the two steps of the Piano, scrambling a little to get the upper one, and she wheeled him round and headed him for the Coffin, managing to check his flat-out speed a little as they approached it. Corny braced himself and slid half-way down the slide and jumped wide and free, but this time when he landed, Dinah was ready – she gathered him in and held him, and they proceeded at a more decorous pace.

They came up into the upper paddock, and Dinah slowed Corny to a controllable canter as she aimed him at the little white fence into the wood. Then the three tricky jumps along the twisty narrow path behind the market garden, and out. Dinah gave Corny his head and spurred him, and he went at the Park Bench with a rush and then was off again. Almost too fast at the in-and-out, but he made it; he jumped too big over the brook and just managed to turn on landing. Dimly, Dinah saw people watching at the water; had there been others along the way? At the Coffin? In the wood? She thought there might have been, but she wasn't sure.

She wasn't really sure of anything except the rush of wind in her hair, the exhilarating tingle of speed, the surge of eager power under her. The Major had said to trot down the long drive here, after the wall, but Corny had other ideas; he went tearing down the long, straight gravel stretch at a hammering gallop, and she could not hold him back; now she did see a blur of faces and waving hats rush past her and behind and away, and she did hear the cheering.

Then, before she knew it, the big Irish bank loomed ahead, and Corny hurled himself, clawing and scrambling, over it, and she put him in and out of the Pen and over the last drop fence back into the show-jumping paddock. She pulled him up, though he was blowing and heaving and throbbing with his eagerness for more.

It's *over*! Dinah thought, and the disappointment was almost more than she could bear; she wanted to cry because it had been so beautiful and it was all gone. She dropped to the ground and loosened Corny's girth: his black neck was shining wet with sweat, his nostrils flaring red, opening and closing, his flanks heaving. He turned his head and nudged her briefly, and Dinah flung her arms round his dripping neck and cried:

'Oh, Corny, I do apologize! You *are* the most wonderful horse in all the world, and I never ever knew it before!'

They didn't all finish the course, and the spectators got their money's worth. Sally had to lead Nightingale in; he quit for good at the Piano. And Blue Trout got away from Enzo and went over the white fence into the wood too fast; he scraped Enzo off on a tree going round the second twist in the narrow path and simply kept right on going, jumping every jump along. Blue Trout loved to jump; he saw no need for carrying anyone along on his back.

Enzo wasn't hurt; he walked home muttering in Italian and ruefully holding the torn seat of his breeches together with his hands. Poor Peanuts was not so lucky. She got clear round the course to the last big Irish bank, the twenty-second jump, and there Pipe Clay fell. Peanuts was thrown clear, but for one stunned second she failed to roll away; in that instant Pipe Clay rolled over to get up, and rolled on Peanuts. Pipe Clay was a very big horse, and Peanuts was a very small girl; it nearly squashed her flat. But somehow when Pipe Clay got up Peanuts still had hold of her reins; very slowly and rather shakily she got to her feet and stood leaning against the big mare, and when people came running to help, Peanuts shook her head and led Pipe Clay away towards the stables herself.

The rest all finished except Cotton Socks, who somehow managed to cast a shoe between the stile and the bales, and who looked vastly pleased with himself as he was led ignominiously away. In all, it was a wonderful morning; the Horsemasters rerode the course horse by horse and jump by jump, over and over again, in the tack-room and at the lunch table, and all through the long sunny afternoon and in the Blue Room until late that night. And Dinah rode it again after that, too, her legs twitching and jerking beneath the bed-clothes as she and Corny P. surged over jump after jump after jump ecstatically.

Chapter 11

Scared to Death

Normally, the cross-country would have been good as a topic for conversation for a good many days, even without the sight of Peanuts limping stiffly about to remind everyone of it a dozen times a day. By noon on Monday, however, they had ceased to talk about it altogether; it was as though it had all happened a long, long time ago.

They had other things on their minds, all of them; they had no time for reliving and relishing an exciting memory. This was the last week – next Monday the B.H.S. Examiner was coming; the Blue Room was packed these evenings with sober, worried-looking students studying their notes or asking one another questions. On Monday, Tuesday, and Wednesday Mr Ffolliott gave his last three quizzes, since Thursday was half-holiday and Friday a free day. And on Monday and Tuesday and Wednesday even the Rides were different, with the Major devoting an hour to perfunctory mounted drills and the remaining hour to calling on the Horsemasters in turn to take over the class and conduct a simulated lesson.

'The Examiner will *definitely* call upon you to do this,' the Major said firmly. 'Your riding will count and your written and oral tests will count, but it is, after all, the Preliminary Instructor's Certificate you are going up for, and the Examiner will *definitely* judge you on your ability to *instruct*. Very well, who's going to give us the lesson on the Sitting Trot? Ah.'

And finally, of course, Friday was to be the Horse Trials, and all through Monday and Tuesday and Wednesday

Red Ride whittled away at Blue Ride's slim lead on the demerit list, until Mercy's record on Wednesday evening showed Blue Ride leading by a slim four points, with the competition scheduled to close at noon on Thursday when Red Ride started on half-holiday.

'One little five-point fine in those stables tomorrow morning, just *one*,' Bee Bye said tensely, 'and we've 'ad it! I'm so nervous, I don't know how I can study tonight!'

'Get up to that Blue Room and get cracking, girl,' Dinah ordered firmly, pushing back her chair. 'I'll be along to join you as soon as David and I have finished night watering. This *would* be my week to draw that extra duty. Come on, David, let's get cracking, shall we? I want to get some studying done!'

Thursday morning started pretty much like any other day in that tense, drawn week; they got down to the stables early and groomed the horses within an inch of their lives, and then meticulously scoured everything they could find. They ate breakfast rather nervously and listened to Mercy read the List almost with apathy; the only unusual thing was the name of a new horse they hadn't heard of before.

'Suzie,' David repeated thoughtfully, 'I'm riding Suzie, am I? And who is Suzie, does anyone know? A charming name for a lady, but –'

'The school bought her last week,' Mercy told him, 'she's down at the Vale stables, of course; you'll have to hack her up with Highboy and Nightshade. I saw her when she arrived; she's a bay, about fifteen hands, quite nice. Jock turned her out for two days to get over her journey, and he's been riding her himself since then; he says she's a bit high-strung but otherwise a very nice ride.'

David nodded, satisfied, and Mercy went on reading the List; that was all that was said about Suzie before the Ride.

Later, when Mercy banged on the feed box and shrilled, 'File out, everybody; file out, please!' Dinah, leading Corny P. out of the stable yard past David and Enzo and Ingrid sitting the three Vale horses and waiting, looked curiously at the trim little bay mare and called, 'How d'you like her, David?'

'She's *lovely*!' David called back, and patted the little bay's neck affectionately. 'Moves *beautifully*, and just charged with enthusiasm! Oh, she's a wonderful ride!'

The Major put them through an hour of mounted drill and halted them; he said briskly:

'All right. Now, we've practised our instructional talks all this week, and we haven't been outside at all; I don't want you to get stale with too much studying. So let's go out and pop over a few small jumps in the top paddock, and have a little fun. File out, and ride up to the upper paddock, and just trot round the big spread fence, the big ditch-and-rails, in a circle. Get their blood up a little . . .'

David rode out first, proudly; the new little mare did seem nervous in the school, but she had gone well for David and he was obviously delighted with her. And she did move beautifully; she was terribly quick and perfectly balanced – the sort of horse that required a good rider to handle her, but responded wonderfully to the right delicate touch. Behind him followed Adrienne on Night Life and then Enzo riding Cotton Socks; Dinah checked Shadow momentarily to let Bee Bye, on the nervous dancing Copper, go ahead of her, and then let Shadow follow on.

The skies were grey with the threat of rain; the reddish earth of the path was still dark with the dew of early morning, although it was eleven o'clock. The sun had not come out to bake it dry and pink. The horses, walking nose to tail in a long file, tossed their heads restlessly and occasionally one or another would break into a shuffling jog for a few steps until his rider checked him firmly, or would dance abruptly sideways out of line, snorting and fighting his bit. There was jumping ahead, and all the horses knew it; the cool moist morning affected them, too, making them restless and unquiet. And of course there were horses like Mayfly or Night Life or Highboy, who were perfectly quiet out alone but always got tense and jumpy in the presence of a lot of other horses, especially outdoors. On a day like this one a mare like Night Life, shying violently every few feet in spite of Adrienne's best efforts to calm her, could communicate her nervousness to all the other horses.

David dismounted to open the gate into the top paddock; he led his little bay mare through and stood holding the gate open while the others filed past him. Adrienne, in the lead, let Night Life begin to trot at once; the graceful black mare steadied down right away and stepped out smartly with a high action, her neck beautifully arched, no longer shying or fighting her bit. Enzo put Cotton Socks into a trot following Adrienne, and Copper broke into a canter for two strides before Bee Bye could check him to the trot; Dinah took a firm hold on Shadow's mouth and touched the grey mare lightly, and Shadow trotted steadily after the others in a wide-swinging circle round and round the oak-fenced wings of the big ditch-and-rails.

Each time Shadow went round the upper side of the circle Dinah could look down across the show-jumping paddock below and over the hedges to the sea, grey and choppy and forbidding-looking beneath the stormy sky; at the bottom of the slope she could glance across the ditch-and-rails to see the riders opposite: Peanuts struggling grimly to keep Blue Trout's nose out of Nutmeg's quarters, Ingrid riding with a firm hold, paying cautious attention to the unpredictable Claddagh Boy. And on the uphill side of the circle Shadow invariably turned her head for an eager look at the dark little wood and the inviting oak post-and-rail jump leading into it.

Then the Major was coming into the paddock, striding briskly through the gate and turning to fasten it behind him, and in that moment the strangled yell of surprise and alarm went up from half a dozen throats behind Dinah. Instinctively she hauled Shadow to an abrupt halt; that yell could only mean someone was in trouble; she had heard it enough times before. As she twisted round in her saddle to see who it was this time, she heard the high clear cry from Jill, rising above all the other voices in shock and dismay and disbelief:

'It's *David*! *David's off!*'

And David *was* off; David the unthrowable, David the expert horseman, David who had ridden out the worst bucking Claddagh Boy or any of the other horses could produce. David, the best of them all by far, the one they had all believed would never come off a horse no matter what happened, was flat on his back on the hoof-marked turf, his legs drawing up as he rolled over to his hands and knees, still holding the reins of the little bay who stood quietly and watched him with alert intelligent eyes.

'What *happened*?' Dinah asked no one in particular, and no one answered her; at first she felt cheated that she had missed seeing it, and then instantly she was deeply sorry for David. He had gone so long with his perfect record, and he rode so well . . .

David put a foot in the stirrup, now, and swung gracefully back into the saddle, and Suzie's head came up attentively, her ears pricked forward as she mouthed her bit. David had a smear of mud on his left cheek bone, standing out dark against the pallor of his set white face; he set himself in the saddle and put his legs gently to the mare – instantly she reared, came down, shot sideways and landed bucking round in a tight, spinning circle with a violence

Dinah had never seen before, nor even imagined. She saw David's head snap back and forth as he clung grimly with hands and knees and body balance, and his hard hat flew off with the jarring violence of Suzie's frenzy, and then Dinah sucked in her breath with a gasp and someone behind her shrieked, and David was diving over Suzie's head, turning over in the air to land on his shoulders and back again with a thud that seemed to shake the earth.

At once Suzie stopped and stood stone-still, regarding him quietly as he lay still for a moment, his breath knocked out of him, and then slowly rolled over and got to his feet again. The little mare stood unmoving as he approached her and put his foot in the stirrup once again, paler than ever, but the Major called out sharply:

'All right, Mr Perrin, that's enough! Two falls from the same horse is all we require from one rider. We'll give someone else a chance! Miss Simms, will you jump down and change with Mr Perrin, please?'

'*Please*, Major Brooke!' David protested violently, in great agitation. '*Please*, sir – let me have another go! I *can* ride her! *Please*, sir!'

The Major hesitated; Bee Bye, with one leg over her saddle ready to drop to the ground, hesitated too. Then the Major nodded curtly; he said quietly:

'Very well, Mr Perrin. Carry on until you feel you've had enough!'

'Thank you, sir!' David called more calmly; steadily he swung up into the saddle, and instantly Suzie exploded once again. She went high in the air and came down hard and jarring, facing in the opposite direction, and instantly went up again; David clung through five incredible furious jolts and came loose; on the seventh he fell once again, this time landing on his feet while Suzie stopped dead still and quiet as she had before.

They watched in round-eyed silent horror while she

threw him twice more; as he got up slowly and approached her to mount for the sixth time, the little mare's forelegs were quivering a bit. She stood quietly while David stroked her nose and crooned to her soothingly; he mounted, and she stood still and attentive. He put his heels to her, and Suzie quivered – and trotted off in docile obedience, picking up her feet smartly, head and tail high.

David trotted once round the circle, while the others sat their horses unmoving; he put Suzie into a high collected canter, and she went quietly round without protest. And he pulled up at last, and said coolly to the Major:

'I think she's come back to me, now. Sorry to hold up the Ride – and thank you, sir!'

A stifled cheer went up from the Horsemasters, and the Major answered dryly:

'You're quite welcome, Mr Perrin. And that was well ridden, very well ridden indeed. Although I suppose –'

He turned, and his eyes sought for Bee Bye and found her, sitting quiet and erect on Copper, watching with enormous eyes; he said, bowing, with a swift mischievous smile flickering across his handsome ruddy face:

'I suppose we must now compliment Miss Simms as the last and only unthrown rider of this Horsemanship Course!'

Bee Bye's face twisted queerly; without a moment's hesitation she drove her heels violently into Copper's sides. And as the startled horse leaped forward, Bee Bye threw herself headfirst out of the saddle, striking the turf with her head and shoulders and rolling while Copper, free, kicked up his heels and pounded off, racing to the far end of the paddock as hard as he could go.

There was a moment of stunned silence as Bee Bye got slowly to her feet, white-faced and shaky. And then the Major, who had turned his back on the Ride to watch the big sorrel galloping round the paddock with loose reins flapping and stirrups swinging empty banging his sides, said in a quiet, conversational tone:

'All right, everyone, just perfectly still, now; he'll come back to the gate. Don't anyone move, or try to catch him . . .'

And Copper did make two circuits of the paddock, looking about him for pursuit; finding none, he stopped dead and trotted easily to the gate and stood there quietly while the Major walked slowly over to him and put out a hand to take his reins.

But Dinah had caught a glimpse of the Major's face as he turned his back on the class; she watched him thoughtfully as he strode off to catch Copper. And she wondered: Now, what on earth do you suppose he was looking so *pleased* about?

And then she noticed that David and Bee Bye were staring silently at each other as though they had never seen each other before, and as Bee Bye suddenly turned her head away and walked off there were two spots of high colour on her cheek bones. *Well!* Dinah thought, *now what do you know about that?*

Dinner had been good, but no one had seemed to have much appetite; even Jill Taylor had failed to yelp, 'Anyone not want theirs?' although she had managed to clear her own plate. And now Mercy Hale was rising, and at once everyone stopped talking; in an expectant hush every head turned to the head of the table.

'By a margin of only seven demerits,' Mercy announced, 'Red Ride has lost, and Blue Ride will go to the Horse Trials tomorrow . . .'

She paused, and a subdued murmur broke out round the table; there was no cheering, and even in her jubilance Dinah did not feel really triumphant, she could not help feeling sorry for the kids on Red Ride who had worked just as hard and had lost.

'I am –' Mercy said hesitantly, and Dinah pricked up her ears at the strange note of warmth in Mercy's high clear voice; it was almost the first sign of emotion Mercy had ever shown, 'I am really sorry you can't *all* go, and so is Major Brooke. You've all worked hard, and worked well, and it's a pity Red Ride can't get off for the day too. But somebody *has* to do the horses. However, Jock Woods will come up to take charge of stables in the morning, and Jock is going to take Red Ride on a long hack, a picnic ride, over some country none of you have seen before. We hope that will make up to some extent for missing the Trials.'

The Red Ride side of the long table perked up at that, and an argument broke out immediately over the desirability of just watching other people ride in the Hunter Trials versus spending a long day actually riding yourself, hacking across country with no one yelling orders at you. Mercy stood still and watched them all quietly for a moment, and Dinah thought the Head Girl's small pale face looked strangely wistful before she moved quietly away from the table and left the room, alone.

'Sure, an' it's generous the Irish are, the lot of 'em,' Betsy Murphy was saying happily, 'an' I'll not be lettin' the rest of 'em down. So I'll change with you, David; I'll go in your place to the Hunter Trials, an' you can hack with our lot. You can ride Suzie, I've no doubt – an' it's certain she's left your ugly face in no shape to show it at Hunter Trials, or all the world'll be after thinkin' they can't teach us to ride here!'

'*Miss* Murphy!' David pronounced with chill formality, smiling lop-sidedly round the great purpling swelling over the left side of his face but still looking deliriously happy, 'you are speaking of the horse I may marry! We –'

Jill whooped with glee, and above the laughter round the table David raised his voice and continued:

'We have an understanding, Suzie and I. And for your information, I *am* going to hack her Saturday morning; I asked the Major, and he promised I could. *There* is a lady of spirit, a lass worthy of a man's adoration – and she has mine! And now come on, Dinah, let's get this night-watering chore over with and perhaps belt the books an hour before sack time, shall we not?'

'Just the same,' Peanuts muttered as Dinah and David rose from the table, 'I shall keep well away from David's new fiancée. And from David – my word, what might she not do if she got jealous, that Suzie?'

In the darkness the stable yard was lonely and deserted, the familiar buildings strange and ominous, looming in great black silhouette against the dark sky. Their footsteps rang loud on the bricks underfoot, echoing in the silence, and Dinah shivered a little although the night was warm. A horse stamped and blew through his nostrils in Stable One; another kicked lightly and tentatively somewhere else; if she strained to listen closely she could hear horses steadily munching hay behind the stable walls, hear the straw bedding rustling with life and motion as they stirred in their stalls.

A switch clicked at David's hand, and warm yellow light flooded out of Stable One, throwing long black shadows on the bricks of the stable yard; his footsteps rang, receding, towards Stable Three, and Dinah went into Stable One to get the empty water buckets there. Nightingale nuzzled her curiously as she slipped past him and groped for his bucket in the straw, and she patted his velvety nose with dispassionate kindness but absently; Corny P. was *her* horse now, and she wouldn't have traded the old black cob for a thousand dark-grey Arabs.

She carried Nightingale's bucket and Blue Trout's out to the water trough and filled them, the clear cold water splashing in a torrent from the shining brass tap. She shut off the tap and carried them back again. She made another trip and that finished Stable One. She came out just as Pipe Clay squealed horribly and David shot out of the big mare's box and slammed the door behind him, bent double in helpless, convulsive laughter.

'Poor old Pipers!' David spluttered, giggling, 'she was lying down when I went in to get her bucket, too comfortable even to get up and go for me. So I got the bucket and took it out and filled it, and when I took it back she was *still* lying down peacefully watching me. And like a silly ass I stepped on her tail, and *then* she nearly had me! Have you finished in One, Dinah?'

'Yes,' Dinah nodded, giggling at the thought of the big mare going for David with those great yellow teeth bared and just missing, 'I was just going to do Two.'

'Well, I've finished Three,' David said. 'We'll do Two together, and that'll be the lot for tonight.'

They went together into Stable Two and David switched on the light and turned to Copper's box; Dinah had her hand on the latch of Cotton Socks's door when they stopped as one and held their breath, listening. The sound was very faint, but it continued; a convulsive sniffling, and then a stifled sob . . .

David moved; he tiptoed silently to the end box, with Dinah close behind him, and together they peered into the shadowy interior. Pennant was stretching her neck to pull a mouthful of hay from the hay net hanging over her manger; she moved away, munching. The sniffling and the sobbing continued; there was a small dark shape huddled in the straw in the shadowy corner of the box.

The latch clanged loudly as David moved, and the door creaked, swinging wide; Dinah followed him in and he closed it and fastened it. The small shape stirred and sat up, and Mercy Hale stared up at them from swollen eyes, her small pale face tear-streaked, her shoulders still shaking uncontrollably. She tried to speak, and could not; she threw herself round and down into the straw again, her whole small body shivering.

Dinah went down on her knees immediately; she touched Mercy's shoulder gently and whispered:

'Mercy. What's the matter?'

Mercy shook her head violently and mumbled indistinctly into the straw:

' 'S nothing. Go 'way, please.'

But David got down on his knees in the straw now, on the other side of Mercy; gently but firmly he pried her face out of the straw, and abruptly Mercy gave in and sat up. David produced a clean handkerchief and held it to Mercy's face, pinching her nose lightly. He murmured with an odd gentleness:

'Come on, Mercy; *blow*!'

Mercy's hand came up and took the handkerchief away from him; she stared at them both helplessly, and then sheepishly turned her head and blew her nose hard and wiped her streaming eyes. Her sobbing stopped and she hiccuped once. David said gently:

'All right, now tell us about it. Please.'

Mercy shook her head violently; then suddenly she blurted shakily:

'I'll *never* get round that course tomorrow. You'll all be watching, *hoping* to see me get thrown, and you'll get your hope! *Nobody* wants to see me pull it off, and I won't; I *can't*; I'm not good enough – you were right about that, David! But I'll disgrace the School; I'll disgrace Pennant and I'll disgrace the School, and everybody'll be glad, and I wish I were *dead*! I *told* the Major I couldn't do it and he w-wouldn't l-listen to m-me.'

She choked and the tears spurted from her eyes again; Dinah put an arm round her and Mercy buried her face in Dinah's neck, her shoulders shaking convulsively again. And David said quietly:

'Of course you can do it, Mercy; the Major wouldn't set you to it if he didn't *know* you could do it, and make the School proud of you. And you're wrong about us; we'll all be rooting for you; we *know* you'll pull it off, and you're *ours*, and we're with you. You have the toughest job there is round this school, Mercy, and it took us all a long time to appreciate how well you do it. But we all know now — *all* of *us*! Please get hold of yourself and get some sleep; you're riding for *all* of us tomorrow. Good night, Mercy, and good luck!'

He got up quickly and gave Dinah his hand and pulled her to her feet; as they hurried out Mercy was sitting up straight and her small square shoulders were erect, her blue eyes wide and staring.

They burst into the Blue Room, and everyone looked up at once from notebooks and texts; even Jill Taylor, toasting herself a slice of bread before the heater, rolled over and sat up, her hunger momentarily forgotten.

'All right, you lot!' David said harshly. 'I'm afraid I have to make a speech, and I want you all to listen to me, please. This has to do with what the Army calls *esprit de corps*, which just means making a ragged bunch of civilians into soldiers who are proud of being part of a good outfit. And even of being with the guy who has the toughest job in the Army – the non-commissioned officer who hammers it into 'em! It isn't the officer in charge who puts *spirit* into his men; it's a good NCO. And the way he does it generally makes him a lonely man everybody else hates – he *has* to make everybody hate him so they'll work hard together against him, and out of their growing together comes the solidarity that makes them part of a team . . .'

He paused and drew a deep breath, his eyes glittering angrily, the bruise on his cheek standing out purple against the tense whiteness of his face. He said crisply:

'All right. We're not the same people we were when we came to this school, any of us. We were just a bunch of lazy, clumsy, slipshod individuals then, and none of us cared about anybody but himself. *Now* we care. *Now* we're all on a team; on two teams, really, but at the same time they're part of the same team; and we're all proud of ourselves and proud of belonging with all the others. We're pretty good, too; we've all learned a lot. How did we get that way?

'We got that way hating Mercy Hale, who made us hate her; we got that way trying to do everything so well she wouldn't be able to find fault with it, just to spite her because we thought it would give her pleasure to find fault. We got that way getting up a little earlier in the morning to get down to the stables before all the good brooms had been taken, to be sure of getting the job done better than somebody would who slept a little later. Did any of you ever suspect that Mercy has a whole dozen brand-new brooms locked up in her supply cupboard? She has – but if she put 'em out for us to use, d'you think we'd get up early and work hard?'

Somebody gasped in astonishment, but all the others watched David in open-mouthed silence as he said:

'She made us compete against one another, in teams, not individually; and she made us all compete against her. She made us so mad at her we'd clean tack at night, and hunt for jobs to do in our free time; she got us to the point where Bee Bye threw herself off her horse this morning because she didn't *want* to be a better rider than another member of her team. A month ago she'd have laughed herself sick if I'd had a fall before she did . . .'

'It wasn't fair!' Bee Bye said suddenly. 'A brand-new horse you'd never even seen before! And she'd 've thrown me, too, only –'

'Shut up!' David said absently and not at all rudely. Then he continued, 'So this is the way it is: the Major's taught us all to ride, the Major and Captain Pinski. But we've *grown up*, too; we've all acquired something even more important than riding skill. And *that* we got from Mercy, and from Mercy alone. And *alone* is just what Mercy is – she's got the loneliest, hardest, most thankless job in the world! She's good at it, but d'you think she enjoys it? She's down in the stable right now bawling her eyes out because she's scared to death about the Trials tomorrow, scared she'll disgrace the School, and lonesome and miserable because she thinks we'll all be glad if she does! So don't you think we might put the books away, and all go down and see if we can't cheer her up a bit?'

After just one frozen, silent, profoundly thoughtful moment they went, in a wild stampede that upset a lamp, two chairs, and a table, and trampled Jill's forgotten toast into the frayed and faded blue rug.

Chapter 12

All Eyes on Mercy

'It *would* rain, of course,' Peanuts said dolefully, huddling into the turned-up collar of a riding mac several sizes too large for her.

Jill Taylor told her cheerfully.

'It *always* rains at Hunter Trials, you little dummy! If the sun ever came out on a day scheduled for horse trials, they'd cancel and postpone the programme while awaiting normal weather. *Doesn't* it look a super course!'

It looked, Dinah thought, a thoroughly forbidding course. Feeling like an expert in the light of her recent experience over the Owen-Allerford cross-country course, she decided critically that you'd have to have your horse under absolute control all the way here. It wasn't that any one of the jumps was any more formidable than those at the School, but the pattern in which the course had been laid out made the jumps positively fiendish. The long gallops approaching such tricky in-and-out jumps as the Pen, which *had* to be taken at moderate speed, would tempt a difficult horse to get out of hand entirely; and then there were several spread jumps like that horrifying ditch-and-rails at the foot of the steep drop, where you'd have to drive your horse for all you were worth to get him at it fast enough to clear it. And of course there was the Quarry, a blood-curdling affair at which you jumped a birch rail and found yourself falling into a grassy pit with precipitous, almost perpendicular sides. You had a sharp turn and another jump in the bottom of the pit and then had to scramble up the other side with what momentum you had left and jump another birch rail at the top – and *then* find yourself and your bewildered horse landing on a steep hillside with a long downhill gallop ahead!

Shivering, Dinah decided that David had been quite right in saying that it might be rather fun to watch a few of the good ones through the Quarry; she was profoundly grateful, though, that she would be watching rather than riding today. She gazed down from the hilltop over the rolling countryside with the crystalline shallow river winding through the valley and the fields neatly fenced with hedges. She counted nine jumps visible from where she stood – a good vantage point from which to watch part of the Trials. To her left, at the bottom of the hill, was the car park; there must have been six or seven hundred cars solidly packed into the level pasture, she thought. And beyond was the line of tents and open-sided caravans selling refreshments of all kinds. Jill Taylor was over there somewhere no doubt. Off to the right were the horse boxes of the competitors, in a roped-off field to themselves; and *everywhere* were people. People in riding macs and people in tweeds, people walking and critically estimating the jumps, and people sitting on shooting sticks watching the other people and absorbedly reading their programmes. And people in black hunting coats and buff breeches and shining black boots and bowlers, with great numeral placards tied to their backs, walking the course alone and in groups and studying the approach to each jump with real concern.

Roger was panting up the hill, threading his way hurriedly through the people on the hillside; he reached the two girls and said breathlessly:

'I say, you lot, our box is here at last! They had a flat tyre, and they're in the most amazing tizzy trying to get ready before they're all disqualified. The Major's gone tearing off to explain all to the judges, Mercy's trying to exercise three horses at once, and the Captain's screaming at everyone in sight. David and Bee Bye and Adrienne are being towers of strength, at least David and Bee Bye are. I think Adrienne's asleep in the horse box. Don't you want to come down and get in on the fun?'

The great clumsy bulk of the dark-green horse van with 'Owen-Allerford Riding School' lettered on its sides and the single word 'Horses' on back and front was parked in a long line of similar vehicles ranging from small one-horse trailers hitched behind the jeep-like Land-Rovers to an incredible thing like a yacht on wheels, all polished mahogany and brass and immaculate white trim. They all had their doors open and ramps down; all over the roped-off Competitors' Paddock were horses saddled and unsaddled, being trotted up and down or led about by grooms. Each little group of people and horses was busy and businesslike and self-absorbed; no one was gawking at anyone else, except for the throngs of spectators staring curiously from the other side of the barrier ropes.

Feeling very professional and superior, the Horse-masters showed their passes and were admitted to the paddock, and went at once to the Owen-Allerford van. Bee Bye and Adrienne were leaning against the ramp as the others came up. Bee Bye said, pointing:

'David's exercising Mayfly over there, and there's Captain Pinski, trotting Bay Rum along the fence, way back. There's Mercy on Pennant – doesn't she look *super*?'

Mercy did, indeed, look quite different in formal black jacket and buff breeches and boots and a hunting stock and bowler; further, her small pale face seemed to have taken on a faint flush of colour, and her features were animated as she cantered Pennant down a short, straight line and stopped her abruptly, and turned and spurted

into the short canter back again. And then they heard
the Major's voice shouting behind them and Mercy
wheeled Pennant and rode towards the horse box with the
Captain close behind her.

The Major came hurriedly towards them; in his hand
he carried three foot-square white placards with competitors' numerals on them in tall black figures and with tapes
dangling from them. Thrusting one at Bee Bye, he said
brusquely:

'Here, Miss Simms, tie this thing on my back, will you?
Someone please take this one and do the same for Mercy,
and this one's for Captain Pinski – *jump*, now! My word,
we've very nearly been disqualified; they're starting off the
Novice Class in fifteen minutes, you know; is Pennant
ready?'

The Major was also a strange and somehow forbidding
figure in formal kit. He was unsmiling and totally pre-
occupied with the business at hand. He thrust his arms
back impatiently to permit Bee Bye to tie the placard
across the back of his black coat. He pulled away restlessly
as soon as she had finished and stamped over to where
Dinah and Adrienne were tying on Mercy's placard while
Jill held the nervous, eager Pennant.

'You haven't even walked the course!' the Major said
fretfully to Mercy, 'and you won't have time to walk it
now. I don't think you ought to ride this course without
walking it first; are you sure you want to, Mercy? Shall we
scratch Pennant? She's entered, but she doesn't have to go;
I've already explained the circumstances to Brigadier Car-
ney who's running the show, and it's entirely up to you.
What do you think?'

Mercy didn't hesitate. She glanced once at the hopeful
encouraging faces of the Horsemasters surrounding her,
nudging her with their eyes. She smiled warmly and said
quite calmly:

'Of *course* we shan't scratch her, Major Brooke. She's ready, and so am I. We go off in pairs, don't we? Then I shall simply hang back behind whoever's paired with me, and go at them as he does, and if his horse clears everything, Pennant will!'

'You're paired with Tom Firr,' the Major said crisply, frowning a little, 'I've known him for years; he's a very steady old gentleman and a sound horseman. I'm not sure of the novice horse he's showing, and neither's Tom, but I've just told him you'd be riding – if you rode at all – without having walked the course. He said jolly good show, and if you've got that kind of guts just to follow him, and he'll do his best to give you a safe lead over. Well, all right, Mercy, off you go. And good luck!'

'Right, thank you, Major Brooke,' Mercy said brightly, still smiling and confident. 'I've seen the map of the course, you know, and we studied the descriptions of the jumps together, and the distances. It shouldn't be too bad, actually. Can I have a leg up, one of you lot?'

Roger got there first, elbowing Jill and Dinah out of his way; he boosted Mercy into her saddle with an enthusiasm that very nearly catapulted her clear over the horse. While she found her stirrups and gathered up her reins, the Horsemasters of Blue Ride called out earnestly:

'You can *do* it, Mercy!' and, 'Good show, Mercy!' and, 'Oh, Mercy, *do* show 'em!' and, 'Come on, Mercy; you and Pennant!' and, 'All the best, Mercy; we're with you!'

Mercy, prepared to depart, looked down at their up-turned earnest faces and smiled a tremulous smile, and said almost inaudibly:

'I – know you are. It'll help, a lot. Well – cheerio, all of you!'

She put her heels to Pennant, and the little mare tossed her head and spurted off in a rocketing canter, settling to a sedate trot as she rounded the roped-off corner into the road and set off for the starting line. Behind her the Horsemasters glanced at one another and, wordless, set off at a hard run for the hilltop to watch the start and the first few jumps.

No one but Dinah seemed to notice that David and Bee Bye hung back a little behind the others and then jogged off holding hands and not trying to catch up. And as soon as Dinah noticed, she legged it as hard as she could to get away from them and leave them alone, as they quite obviously wanted to be. They had, as a matter of fact, been together almost constantly ever since the day David had come off Suzie and Bee Bye had thrown herself off Copper; David's speech in the Blue Room that night might have been right in every other respect, but he hadn't entirely understood Bee Bye's reasons for taking a voluntary fall. Not *then*, he hadn't . . .

Next to the tent on the top of the hill with the 'Secretary' sign outside stood an open truck painted olive drab with a set of four loudspeakers mounted on it, pointing in four directions. There were two civilians and a British soldier standing clustered round the loudspeakers, and one of the civilians held a hand microphone; a second soldier, wearing earphones and holding in his lap a black box festooned with wires, perched on the roof of the truck's cab.

Looking off across the valley, Dinah could see, now, other little groups of soldiers in uniform sprawled in the grass and in the ploughed fields and huddled under hedges; she could not see clearly what they were doing, but they seemed to have some sort of field radio equipment, and she surmised that they were walkie-talkie radio teams reporting to the men on the loudspeaker truck.

The loudspeaker interrupted her train of thought; it squawked once or twice as though clearing its throat, and announced in a metallic mechanical voice:

'Class One, the Novice Hunter Trial, is about to begin. The first pair of competitors will be Spearmint, owned by Mrs Clayton Hall and ridden by Miss Beverly Miles, and Black Pirate, owned and ridden by Sir Adrian Greville. They're *off*!'

Standing on tiptoe, bouncing up and down and bobbing her head to see over the people in front of her, Dinah finally found the two horses far away in the distant paddock, two specks crawling slowly and steadily side by side to the edge of the field and suddenly soaring into the air to hang suspended there for a moment and come gracefully to earth again in the next field. And now they were turning, coming directly towards her, growing larger and larger; a tall black horse a little in the lead, a shorter, stubbier chestnut keeping pace a length behind, and the two black-coated riders half-standing in their stirrups, crouched low over the horses' necks.

'Black Pirate is safely over the drop fence,' the squawk box said abruptly. 'Now Spearmint is safely over; they are in the straight at a hard gallop towards the Pen ...'

Dinah saw the big black thundering towards the Pen, and heard Roger at her elbow suck in his breath; she knew the horse was going too fast to negotiate the in-and-out jump safely and clenched her fists until her nails bit into her palms. And then at the last moment the black horse's rider, unable to check his mount's speed, managed to turn him; the black veered sharply away from the Pen and his rider brought him round in a sweeping circle to approach it again at a more moderate speed. The stubby chestnut horse had checked almost to a halt, jumped into the Pen and out again, and at once flattened out into a gallop; he was now far ahead.

'Spearmint is through the Pen and approaching the stile-in-wire,' the loudspeaker squawked. 'Black Pirate is

charged with a refusal at the Pen. Black Pirate is now
through the Pen and coming on . . .'

'Come on!' Roger said urgently, 'if we run we can get
to the Quarry ahead of this pair; the black's going to be in
trouble there.'

The chestnut swerved hard away from the stile built in
the middle of an unobstructed field, charging for the wire
which was actually only painted string at one side of it;
the girl riding him managed to swerve him back in time,
however, and the chestnut leaped the stile without checking his pace. The black horse was coming up hard, but
Dinah turned away and ran with the rest for the top of
the next hill, and the Quarry.

The black horse was just behind the chestnut as they
came hammering up the steep hillside; the chestnut took
the oak post-and-rails at the top of the hill just ahead of
the black, and they came up to the birch rail at the lip
of the Quarry almost together, and soared over it without
checking speed. And they slid frantically clawing and
scrambling for footing down the steep side of the pit while
their riders clung like monkeys to their backs; somehow
the horses recovered their balance enough to jump the
rail at the bottom, and together they clawed and
scrambled up the almost-perpendicular slope at the opposite side, and hurled themselves over the remaining fence
to vanish beneath the slope beyond.

Dinah let out her pent-up breath with an explosive
sigh, and heard its echo three times at her elbow. The
squawk box cleared its throat and remarked mildly:

'Spearmint and Black Pirate are both safely through the
Quarry.'

Bee Bye began to giggle helplessly then; when they all
turned to look at her inquiringly, she protested defen-
sively:

'You *English*! If someone said he had a horse who

could walk on water, and offered to ride him across the Thames to prove it, your reporter covering the event would simply remark, "The gentleman has successfully gained the opposite bank of the Thames," and let it go at that!'

David looked at her coldly.

'An American would undoubtedly think of a great deal more to *say*,' he said aloofly, 'but that would be the gist of the matter. I say, they've both done it safely, the whole lot; they're in the flat! Do look!'

The black and the chestnut were indeed over the last fence and galloping flat out over the long straight towards the twin red finishing flags. The loudspeaker said without emotion:

'Spearmint and Black Pirate have finished the course. The next pair to start will be Rajah, owned and ridden by Major A. R. J. Glidden-Leigh, and Wood Sprite, owned by the Welkin Stables and ridden by Mrs Robert Farnow.'

'I'm starved!' Jill whispered loudly. 'Standing about in the air *does* give one a fearful appetite, doesn't it? Can't we go down to one of those caravans and have a sausage roll?'

'Eat your packed lunch,' Peanuts told her heartlessly. 'You've got it in the pocket of your mac. And when did *you* have to stand in the air to whet your appetite, Hungry?'

'Well, standing in the rain is getting me wet,' Dinah said unhappily, and sneezed, 'and if Mercy isn't due to appear for a while yet *I'll* go with you, Jill, just to get dried off so I won't miss seeing her on acount of being in the hospital with pneumonia. How much time have we got?'

'Mercy is Number Thirteen,' David said, and consulted his watch, 'which should make her the seventh pair. And that pair took just under eight minutes, so you should have rather better than half an hour before she goes off. It *does* look like the weather's clearing a little, and there are forty-one entries in the Novice Class alone, before we even get to the Open where the real fun is. D'you know, I believe I'll come and have a cup of tea with you! Anyone else?'

The skies did not exactly clear, but by the time they emerged from the shelter of the awning canopy before the refreshment caravan's long counter, the rain had slowed to a fine mist that could hardly be called even a drizzle, and the sky was perceptibly lighter in colour. Slipping and stumbling in the wet grass, the seven Horsemasters scrambled back up the slope to the Quarry, from which point they had decided they could best watch Mercy and Pennant over most of the course.

'We shall miss seeing her through the Pen,' David said regretfully, 'and that's rather a chancy approach for Mercy to take with a puller like Pennant. But if we see the Pen, we shall miss the river, and that's a devilish tricky thing; we missed it last time, running to get over here.'

The loudspeaker cleared its throat once again; it sputtered once or twice, and remarked:

'Maundy Money and Elspeth have finished the course. The next pair to start will be Tom's Fool, owned and ridden by Colonel Sir Thomas Firr, and Pennant, owned by the Owen-Allerford Riding School and ridden by Miss Mercy Hale.'

Peanuts jabbed Dinah in the ribs with her elbow, jumping up and down excitedly; unable to contain herself, Dinah grabbed Bee Bye round the waist and spun her round in an exuberant waltz. Then she became aware of the coolly lifted eyebrows of the bystanders, and sheepishly slunk back to her place, staring straight ahead with flaming ears. Just behind her a woman's voice was saying loudly and clearly:

'But it's a *wonderful* school, darling, they say it's the best in England! And their horses are *superbly* conditioned; Tony Christian had one from them two seasons back, you remember that enormous grey he hunted all winter and then sold for some preposterous price?'

'Paid a preposterous price, too, as I recall,' a man's voice drawled, and the woman's voice countered:

'But they've entered this little mare as a Novice, and she doesn't look up to weight. I *do* think, if she does well over the course, we might look at her for Gillian. She'd be so *thrilled* to have an Owen-Allerford horse!'

The loudspeaker whistled, drowning out the man's reply; Dinah's chest swelled with pride as the squawk box announced:

'Tom's Fool and Pennant have started, and are over the first fence ...'

'I can't *bear* it!' Peanuts squealed ecstatically. 'Oh, come *on*, Mercy!'

A *wonderful* school, Dinah thought. The best riding school in England. Oh, lady, you are so right!

'Tom's Fool and Pennant are over the second fence,' the squawk box remarked, 'and going hard for the Pen. They are checking. Tom's Fool is into the Pen and out. Pennant is into the Pen, and out ...'

'*She did it!*' David whispered prayerfully. 'She's holding her, keeping her back of the other chap, letting him set the pace. Oh, *good*! If she can just hold that horse *in*!'

'Tom's Fool and Pennant are approaching the stile-in-wire,' the loudspeaker said. 'They are both over the stile-in-wire and over the bank into the road ... they are coming out of the road approaching the river ...'

'*There they are!*' Adrienne squealed, jumping up and down and pointing quite unnecessarily as the two horses came into view, a tall rangy bay leading and Pennant a half-length behind. They galloped straight at the river, passing between the two flags that marked the course, and checked; the tall bay took one forward bound into the water and strode boldly towards the opposite shore with Pennant hard on his heels. The river was neither broad nor deep at this point; the water did not reach above the horses' knees.

Tom's Fool reached the opposite bank and scrambled out of the water; he was confronted immediately by a stout oak post-and-rail fence, which had been fiendishly placed a half-stride from the water's edge. Colonel Sir Thomas Firr spurred his young horse hard, and Tom's Fool leaped valiantly, jumping off his hocks – and an involuntary cry went up from the crowd as he hit the top rail hard and fell, spilling Colonel Sir Thomas on to the wet grass in a confused welter of waving upturned horse's legs and black boots and white breeches and flapping stirrups as horse and rider rolled over and struggled to their feet.

Mercy, hard on Sir Thomas's heels, had no chance to check Pennant as the little mare struggled out of the shallow water; she drove the mare hard at the fence and Pennant made a prodigious effort and cleared it, managing somehow to avoid landing on either the fallen horse or his rider. And while Sir Thomas and Tom's Fool were still scrambling to their feet, Pennant was half a field away and going hard. Then, to Dinah's vast relief, they slowed as Mercy somehow found the strength to haul the eager little mare back to a mild canter.

'Tom's Fool has fallen at the river,' the loudspeaker said, 'but his rider has remounted and is continuing the course. Pennant is safely over the river but is checking speed to wait for Tom's Fool. Pennant's rider was late arriving and has not walked the course; she is relying on Tom's Fool for a lead over. Tom's Fool has caught up and both horses are going well across the flat approaching the Quarry . . .'

'Fancy riding *this* course without even walking it first!' the same woman exclaimed behind Dinah. 'They *must* turn out some Cossacks at that school!'

'Turn out some rather decent-looking horses, too, at that,' the man's voice conceded judiciously. 'I *do* like the appearance of this little chap. Perhaps we shall have a look at her later!'

'Squaw-wk-k!' said the loudspeaker, 'Tom's Fool and Pennant are at the Quarry . . .'

The tall bay bounded over the brow of the hill with Pennant a length behind; one after the other they gathered themselves and jumped the oak post-and-rails and approached the birch rail at the lip of the Quarry quite slowly, at a well-collected canter. Tom's Fool jumped into the Quarry, and then Dinah had a rushing glimpse of Mercy's face, flushed and intent but alive and smiling, as little Pennant soared over the birch and slithered down the wall of the pit in a cascade of loose earth and bouncing pebbles, cleared the bottom fence in a great catlike bound, and rushed at the other side.

'Tom's Fool and Pennant,' the squawk box remarked, 'are through the Quarry . . .'

'She goes well,' the man's voice behind Dinah remarked thoughtfully, 'although of course that girl shows her to advantage; she's a jolly good rider. I do rather like the look of the little mare . . .'

'Come on!' David urged, catching Dinah's arm. 'Let's spring back to the box and be there when Mercy comes in. We can walk Pennant round to cool her out, and generally lend a hand, and still see the last of the Novices before lunch. And *then* the fun begins, when the Captain and the Major go belting off in the Open! But *didn't* Mercy go well?'

Breathless, Dinah could only nod as they slithered down the slippery slope; at the bottom, though, she said hesitantly:

'David. Those people behind us. They were talking about *buying* Pennant!'

'My dear innocent,' David said, and stopped to thrust his open programme under her nose, pointing to the list of entries, 'that's what she's here for; that's one way the School makes money, by showing horses to advantage and selling at a profit.'

The listing was there, all right; at the top of the long column of horses' names and owners was the line that said, '(*) Indicates horse for sale.' And below, among the others, were the Owen-Allerford entries: *Bay Rum, *Mayfly, *Pennant.

'Poor Mercy!' Dinah whispered.

Chapter 13

The Final Bid

Behind the rail of the Visitors' Gallery at the end of the Covered School the Examiner sat lean and grey and attentive, leaning a little forward over a small table, his head inclined towards Captain Pinski, beside him, as his sharp eyes watched the riders circling the walls below. The Major stood spruce and erect in the centre of the school, watching only the riders as he barked his crisp commands; never once did he glance up at the gallery where the Examiner occasionally whispered a question to the Captain, occasionally scribbled something on the sheets of paper laid out on the table before him. Except for the creak of saddles and the muffled thudding of the horses' hooves and the Major's crisp commands, there was no sound in the Covered School, only the tense hush that almost breathed . . .

Her father's letter cracked in the inside pocket of Dinah's hacking jacket as she inclined her body a little inward, bending Corny P. precisely round a corner, and straightened; a spot of warmth seemed to spread from it, giving her a serene confidence. She kept her eyes rigidly looking straight ahead between Corny's up-pricked ears, her attention alertly fixed on the Major's voice; she was aware of the Examiner's presence, but it didn't seem to trouble her now that The Day was here.

You seem to feel that perhaps you may fail to pass your Examination, (*her father's letter said*) and from your description it does appear to cover a formidable area of knowledge for you to have learned in a single summer. We hope you will pass, of course, but we won't be disappointed in you one bit if you do fail; and I hope you won't be disappointed if you find yourself at State instead of Wells.

Considering the change that has taken place in you during this summer, Dinah, I don't think you will. Whether you pass the Examination or not, your gamble has been a successful one; you have set yourself a very difficult task and worked harder at it than I should ever have believed you – or any girl of your age, brought up as you have been – would be capable of working at anything. Your letters show us that you have learned a great deal more than you set out to learn – that you have learned to rise to a challenge and to accept responsibility, that you have grown and matured. Whatever your showing in the Examination, your thousand dollars has been well spent, and so has your summer.

Your mother and I are very proud of you, Dinah, and *very* impatient to have you back at home again. Good luck, and ...

The Major slapped his boot with his stick and cleared his throat; he called crisply:

'From Mr Nicholson as leading file ... *Num———ber!*'

'One!' Roger barked smartly, snapping his head to the right, and instantly Bee Bye's voice yelped, 'Two!' and the clipped shouts travelled back along the line of trotting horses, 'Three!' 'Four!' 'Five!' ... Adrienne snapped her head smartly to the right and yelped, 'Eleven!' and Dinah promptly shouted, 'Twelve!' and heard 'Thirteen!' and 'Fourteen!' ring out behind her.

'Numbers One through Seven,' the Major barked, 'are designated Number One ride; Numbers Eight through Fourteen, Number Two Ride ... Number One Ride, across the school, right ... *tur-r-rn!*'

Along the long side of the school the first seven horses turned smartly inwards and trotted abreast in a long even row across the vast arena, while the following seven continued on round the wall in single file.

'Number One Ride ...' the Major called, and paused to

time his command exactly, 'in the track, left . . . *tur-r-rn!*'

The row of seven trotted almost into the wall and turned smartly left, and became a single file trotting briskly towards a head-on collision with the second seven, now rounding the corner into the short end of the school just in front of the Visitors' Gallery.

'Number One Ride, at the C marker, left *turn!*' the Major shouted, 'and Number Two Ride, at the C marker, *right* turn!'

Copper and Night Life came face-to-face at the C marker in the middle of the short end; Roger swung Copper smartly into a sharp left turn and Betsy Murphy simultaneously bent Night Life to the right. And as the following horses did the same, the two single files of riders became a double file, trotting two abreast down the middle of the school. And now the Major increased the tempo of his barked commands, and the riders crossed and recrossed the big arena trotting and cantering, four abreast and then two abreast again; and then four abreast riding in one direction and passing through four abreast riding in the other; and then two abreast in a serpentine; until finally the Examiner interrupted, calling out clearly:

'Very well, Major Brooke, that will do! You are not required to turn out a military drill team, you know! I will pass your entire class on this phase of their riding here and now, with highest compliments to them and to you, and I have no doubt at all that they will perform equally well in the jumping later on! But we are running short of time this morning, and this is an instructor's course; I should like to hear how they go about instructing. Let's start off with . . .'

He paused and held a whispered consultation with Captain Pinski, then said pleasantly:

'Miss Wilcox. Which of you is Miss Wilcox? Ah. Very

well, Miss Wilcox, I want you to pretend that this is a class you have started as beginners, that you have got them satisfactorily up through the sitting trot and are ready to introduce them to the rising trot. Come forward, Miss Wilcox, face your class, and have at it!'

Dinah's throat went suddenly dry and closed up tight with panic; she could not remember ... And then, as she spurred Corny forward out of line, the letter in her pocket crackled reassuringly, and she swallowed hard and felt suddenly all right. She turned Corny and halted him, facing the long silent row along the wall; she gave him loose rein and Corny dropped his head to stretch his neck. They were all looking at her soberly, waiting, but not quite *at* her; their eyes pretended to be fixed on her but actually looked just past her. *They're all helping me!* Dinah thought gratefully, and then, *And this is what it'll be like at Wells!*

'Good morning, Class,' she began, and was pleased to discover that her voice came out clearly without a quaver; with growing confidence, as the rehearsed lessons came back to her, she went on pleasantly, 'Now that you have learned to sit firmly down in your saddles at the trot without being too badly shaken up, we are ready to try the *second* method of riding at the trot: rising. Rising, or posting, is more comfortable and less tiring both for you and for your horse, and if you watch me now I will demonstrate how it looks before I say any more about it ...'

She spurred Corny P. into his bone-jarring trot and sat to it for two or three strides, and then bent slightly forward and began to rise lightly and rhythmically as she brought him round the school back to his place, and halted.

'Now,' she said seriously, absorbed – she had almost forgotten that this was not a *real* class of beginners – 'there are several things I hope you noticed. First, you do not begin rising until your horse is trotting fairly; when you ask him for the trot and he responds, you sit down in the saddle for several strides and *then* begin to rise. Second, your rising motion is *forward* as well as *upwards*. Third, you should rise no higher than is necessary just to get your weight out of the saddle on alternate strides. Fourth, you rise from your knees and thighs as well as from your stirrups – later we will practise rising to the trot *without* stirrups, to develop the feeling of independent lower legs and feet. And finally, you must *never* on *any* account pull yourself up by the reins. Now, there are several *wrong* ways to rise at the trot, several common mistakes; I will show you what they look like . . .'

She collected Corny P. and sent him on again, calling out as he trotted round the school, 'I am now rising too high and too straight – this forces my horse to increase his pace, and it's uncomfortable for both of us. And now my body is bent too far forward and I am losing contact with my horse's mouth . . .'

She returned to her place and halted again, and as she opened her mouth to speak, the Examiner called out:

'That will do very well, Miss Wilcox, very well indeed. Will you rejoin the Ride, please, and let's have – let me see . . .'

By the time he had finished calling on each of the Horsemasters for a short instructional address, and then had ordered them out into the jumping paddocks and put each in turn over a short course of jumps, it was after noon. Dismissed for the morning, they raced through quartering the horses, fed them, and sprinted to answer the gong for lunch, leaving their tack uncleaned.

Immediately after lunch, without a break of any kind, came the dreaded Written Examination. The Examiner

sat at the head of the cleared dining-room table and passed
out mimeographed question sheets, looked at his watch
and commanded:

'All right, you have an hour and a half. Go!'

Dinah shut her eyes and murmured a silent prayer;
she opened them again, and looked at the first question.
It said:

'Give the symptoms, causes and treatment of:

  (*a*) Thrush.

  (*b*) Flatulent colic.

  (*c*) Lampas.'

Her eyes widened incredulously and then raced down
the sheet, swiftly reading the questions that followed. And
with a smile of relief and pure delight she bent her head
over her paper and began to write as fast as she could,
pouring out the answers without hesitation or doubt.

The Examiner gathered up the papers and the question
sheets, and stuffed them into his attaché case. He said
crisply:

'All right, now for the last part. Let's go down to your
tack-room and your stables, and we'll see how you are on
General Knowledge. This will be just a little informal
discussion, nothing to be afraid of – not that I think any
of *you* lot are much afraid of anything!'

He perched himself on the bench beneath the tack-
room window, swinging his legs idly as Jock Woods always
did, and his comfortable informality put them all at their
ease at once. He said cheerfully:

'All right, now I'm going to ask you all questions about
anything that pops into my head, and we'll see what kind
of answers we get. You'll have to clean all this tack later
on, won't you? Why don't you get on with it now? No
reason you can't be working while we're talking, if you
like ...'

I *do* want something to do with my hands! Dinah thought at once, and went for Corny's bridle. And presently the tack-room was full of Horsemasters assiduously cleaning bridles and saddles, while they listened attentively to the Examiner asking casual questions, going from one to another, and quite unobtrusively making little check marks on the sheets attached to his clipboard.

He asked Adrienne what she would look for in buying oats and hay, and he asked Sally when she would put a horse in a Pelham bridle; he asked David to describe the steps to take in getting a horse ready to turn out to grass at the end of the hunting season, and Peanuts how and at what time of year she would clip her horse on bringing him in. He asked Jill what steps she would take to correct overreach, and he asked Enzo Lalli how he would determine whether a sudden lameness was in the shoulder or the foot. He went on asking questions seemingly at random and very casually, and as each in turn was called upon, he paused in his work and answered thoughtfully but without hesitation.

Finally the Examiner picked up his clipboard and got slowly down from the bench; he looked round at the lot of them and smiled, and shook his head and said approvingly:

'You're a bright lot, you are! I shouldn't tell you this, until I've had a chance to grade your Written papers, but I *will* tell you right now: even if you've missed the Written completely, and I don't for a moment believe that any of you have, you'll *all* pass solely on the basis of your riding, your general knowledge, and your aptitude for teaching. My congratulations to all of you, and to Owen-Allerford School!'

He nodded cordially and strode out, and as one they whooped with delight and relief. And then David said suddenly:

'My *word*! D'you know it's just on five o'clock? And we haven't fed, or bedded down, or done the yards – let's get on with it!'

They went out of the tack-room in a wild rush, and stopped. There in the doorway was Mercy Hale, wiping a stray lock of white-blonde hair back from her pale, damp forehead; Dinah thought that she had never in her entire life seen anyone look so completely exhausted.

'It's all done,' Mercy said weakly. 'I've fed your horses, and bedded down, and done the yards. Everything's finished. Let's all go up to tea; I *need* a cup of tea!'

There was a moment of stunned and absolute silence, while Dinah tried to grasp the picture of one small girl silently driving herself through all their work alone, and then Bee Bye gasped:

'*Fourteen horses! Alone!* Oh, *Mercy*, you – you little –!'

And suddenly Bee Bye was crying, digging her knuckles into her eyes and then hugging Mercy hard, and everything looked kind of misty to Dinah, too, and she could hear someone sniffling beside her.

The conversation in the Blue Room was desultory: nobody seemed to have anything much to say. They were a dejected-looking lot, sprawled about the familiar shabby room; no one seemed to be able to look at anyone else. And the same thought lay unspoken in all of them: it was over, finished and done with, the Horsemasters no longer existed as a group. Their bags were packed, their rooms already looked bare and empty and deserted; they could protest desperately, 'We'll meet again; it isn't *for ever*!' But it *was* for ever, and they knew it; it would never be like this, all together, again.

Peanuts's parents were arriving in the morning to take her back to Sussex; Ingrid would drive with them to London and fly from there to Oslo and her home. Bee Bye and

Dinah would have two days in London, too, and then fly to New York. Gretel was packed and ready to return to Amsterdam; Enzo had his reservations for Genoa. Adrienne would be in Lausanne tomorrow night ...

Dinah got up abruptly; her eyes were stinging, and she did not want to look at Jill, morosely toasting her inevitable bit of bread, nor at Peanuts, looking so wistful and dejected, nor at Roger, staring out of the window at the sea as though he had never seen it before. To think that she would never see any of them again –

'I'm going down to the stables,' she said, and choked a little, 'and see how C-Corny P.'s getting along. I don't know *who's* going t-take care of him now.'

'Somebody will,' Bee Bye said morosely, and it was no consolation to Dinah; she could only think, yes, somebody would – there'd be another new class of Horsemasters arriving the end of this week. But how long would it take Somebody Else to get over resenting Corny P. for his untidiness and his clumsiness and realize that he was the most wonderful old horse that ever lived? How long would he be disliked and tolerated before somebody loved him again? She dragged herself dispiritedly towards the door, feeling empty and sick, and suddenly the door opened and David burst in, and at the violence of his arrival everyone looked up at once.

'*Listen!*' David said, in great agitation. 'You know those people who were standing behind us at the Hunter Trials, the ones who were talking about buying Pennant for their horrible daughter? Well, they're *here*; they've come with a whacking great horse box, and they're out in the stables right now, haggling about price with the Major! But they look like having all the money in England, and they brought their box; they don't mean to go off without her!'

'But –' Peanuts squeaked, and her eyes were horrified,

'but they *can't* sell *Pennant*! Pennant's *Mercy's* horse! Why, it would – it would break Mercy's heart if they sold her!'

The murmur rose from all of them at once; dismayed and protesting and angry. Roger got off the window-sill and advanced a step into the room; Jill dropped her toast and got slowly to her feet; Enzo cocked his fists on his hips and scowled, his face black with fury. And Dinah's heart was suddenly light as she looked round at the others; it *wasn't* over, quite; for just this minute, right now, the Horsemasters were solidly together again!

And then Bee Bye was up, dragging her wallet out of her pocket, saying to all of them in a harsh, shaking tone of voice that wasn't like Bee Bye's voice at all:

'Of course they can't! How *could* the Major –? Listen, David, you can talk to the Major, you've *got* to! You tell him *whatever* price those people will pay we'll make it up somehow; I'll cable my father; I'll *make* him see. You give him this for a – a down payment, so he'll know we mean it; I didn't really want to buy any c-clothes in L-London! I want to buy Pennant for Mercy! *Hurry*, David! You're the only one who can face up to the Major; I'd j-just bust out bawling!'

'Wait a minute!' Jill yelped exultantly. 'Hold it there, boy! *I* don't need all this stuff either!'

Swiftly she spread a vast silk bandanna in the middle of the Blue Room rug, and emptied her wallet on to it; fishing in her pockets she cascaded a handful of coins on top of two pound notes and a 50p piece. And suddenly it began to rain money on to Jill's bandanna as, one by one, the Horsemasters crowded in, elbowing one another out of the way and piling what money they had atop the heap. And then they stood back, flushed and bright-eyed and breathless, and looked at the pile with pride and then with swift-growing doubt.

'Probably thirty-five pounds in all,' Roger said quietly, 'maybe forty. Pennant's probably worth three hundred.'

'We'll *get* the rest!' Bee Bye said fiercely. 'Somehow! *Hurry*, David!'

'*Right!*' David said suddenly, crisply; he bent and gathered up the corners of the bandanna and whirled and ran out of the room, and was gone.

And now they could look at one another again; the Course was still over, and they were still breaking up in just a few hours, but for now they were together again; they were still the Horsemasters of Owen-Allerford.

'My father will wish to help in this,' Adrienne murmured, 'he will like this idea, I think, very much!'

'I will telephone,' Enzo said decisively. 'In Genoa I have money, I have shares of stock in my father's company. I will pay *all* if anyone wishes!'

'No one wishes, you idiot!' Peanuts said rudely. 'You'll pay your share and not a lira more and be glad of the privilege. *I* shall draw my allowance in advance for the rest of this year; my mother will be delighted to let me do it!'

'Three hundred pounds,' Betsy Murphy murmured sombrely, 'is an awful lot of money. But –'

And then suddenly the Major was standing in the Blue Room doorway, surveying them all with his frosty blue eyes, and every voice was stilled. In the silence the Major took two deliberate steps into the room, with David close on his heels; the Major halted with military precision, and David halted a half-step behind him.

'The school has just received two bids for the mare Pennant,' the Major announced crisply. 'One, from a Mr Forbes-Wallace of Newquay, in Cornwall, of three hundred and seventy-five pounds; and the other, from certain agents representing the interests of one Miss Mercy

Hale, of – ah – thirty-seven pounds eighty-four pence . . .'

The Major coughed, and his frosty blue eyes seemed to be watering; he blew his nose violently and stuffed his handkerchief back into his pocket. Then he continued in his clipped precise voice:

'It is a part of the Owen-Allerford School's business to school horses for sale at an advantageous price. Of course you all know that. But it is also a part of the School's policy, when considering an offer for a horse it has for sale, to take into consideration the kind of home to which the horse will be going. In this case, as I have just explained with some difficulty to Mr Forbes-Wallace, the School does not feel the horse would be sufficiently happy with him to warrant consideration of his – ah – appreciably higher bid . . . *and so the horse is not going anywhere!*'

For an incredulous moment they were silent, and then they began to shriek and hug one another deliriously, while the Major collapsed into helpless laughter, wiping his eyes and choking:

'Thirty-seven pounds eighty-four pence! Oh, my *word*, what a splendid price for a horse like Pennant!'